# Tangled With You

# Also From J. Kenner

**Fallen Saint Series:**
My Fallen Saint
My Beautiful Sin
My Cruel Salvation
Sinner's Game

**Stark Security:**
Shattered With You
Broken With You
Ruined With You
Wrecked With You
Destroyed With You
Memories of You
Ravaged With You
Hidden With You
Charmed By You
Tangled With You

**The Stark Saga:**
Release Me
Claim Me
Complete Me
Anchor Me
Lost With Me
Damien
Enchant Me
Interview With The Billionaire

**Stark Ever After:**
Take Me
Have Me
Play My Game
Seduce Me
Unwrap Me
Deepest Kiss
Entice Me

Hold Me
Please Me
Indulge Me
Delight Me
Cherish Me
Embrace Me

**Stark International Steele Trilogy:**
Say My Name
On My Knees
Under My Skin
Take My Dare (novella, includes bonus short story: Steal My Heart)

**Stark World Standalone Stories:**
Justify Me **(part of the Lexi Blake Crossover Collection)**

**Jamie & Ryan Novellas:**
Tame Me
Tempt Me
Tease Me

**Dallas & Jane (S.I.N. Trilogy):**
Dirtiest Secret
Hottest Mess
Sweetest Taboo

**Most Wanted:**
Wanted
Heated
Ignited

**Wicked Nights:**
Wicked Grind
Wicked Dirty
Wicked Torture

**Man of the Month:**
Down On Me
Hold On Tight

Need You Now
Start Me Up
Get It On
In Your Eyes
Turn Me On
Shake It Up
All Night Long
In Too Deep
Light My Fire
Walk The Line
Royal Cocktail
Bar Bites: A Man of the Month Cookbook

**Blackwell-Lyon:**
Lovely Little Liar
Pretty Little Player
Sexy Little Sinner
Tempting Little Tease

**Also by Julie Kenner**

**Demon Hunting Soccer Mom Series:**
Carpe Demon
California Demon
Demons Are Forever
Deja Demon
The Demon You Know
Demon Ex Machina
Pax Demonica
Day of the Demon
How to Train Your Demon

**The Dark Pleasures Series:**
Caress of Darkness
Find Me in Darkness
Find Me in Pleasure
Find Me in Passion
Caress of Pleasure

**Rising Storm:**
Tempest Rising
Quiet Storm

# Tangled With You
## A Stark Security Novella
### By J. Kenner

1001 DARK NIGHTS
PRESS

Tangled With You
A Stark Security Novella
By J. Kenner

Copyright 2023 Julie Kenner
ISBN: 979-8-88542-017-4

Published by 1001 Dark Nights Press, an imprint of Evil Eye Concepts, Incorporated

All rights reserved. No part of this book may be reproduced, scanned, or distributed in any printed or electronic form without permission. Please do not participate in or encourage piracy of copyrighted materials in violation of the author's rights.

This is a work of fiction. Names, places, characters and incidents are the product of the author's imagination and are fictitious. Any resemblance to actual persons, living or dead, events or establishments is solely coincidental.

# A Note From the Author

For years, I've been wanting to tell Ollie's story, but could never seem to find the right woman for him. I wondered if maybe he and Courtney needed to reconcile, but that never felt right. So I started keeping an eye out, paying attention to the characters who appeared in Stark World, thinking that surely he'd find someone. And then one day I was working on one of the Stark Security books, and low-and-behold, Ollie and Trevor were becoming friends. Except it was more than just friends. There was that spark, you know? And that's when I realized that Ollie's perfect match was a guy. More than that, his perfect match was the guy who had over time become his best friend. Once I realized that, everything clicked. All that had to happen was for Ollie to get comfortable with himself. I hope you enjoy going on that journey with him!

# One Thousand and One Dark Nights

*Once upon a time, in the future…*

*I was a student fascinated with stories and learning. I studied philosophy, poetry, history, the occult, and the art and science of love and magic. I had a vast library at my father's home and collected thousands of volumes of fantastic tales.*

*I learned all about ancient races and bygone times. About myths and legends and dreams of all people through the millennium. And the more I read the stronger my imagination grew until I discovered that I was able to travel into the stories… to actually become part of them.*

*I wish I could say that I listened to my teacher and respected my gift, as I ought to have. If I had, I would not be telling you this tale now. But I was foolhardy and confused, showing off with bravery.*

*One afternoon, curious about the myth of the Arabian Nights, I traveled back to ancient Persia to see for myself if it was true that every day Shahryar (Persian: شهریار, "king") married a new virgin, and then sent yesterday's wife to be beheaded. It was written and I had read that by the time he met Scheherazade, the vizier's daughter, he'd killed one thousand women.*

*Something went wrong with my efforts. I arrived in the midst of the story and somehow exchanged places with Scheherazade – a phenomena that had never occurred before and that still to this day, I cannot explain.*

*Now I am trapped in that ancient past. I have taken on Scheherazade's life and the only way I can protect myself and stay alive is to do what she did to protect herself and stay alive.*

*Every night the King calls for me and listens as I spin tales. And when the evening ends and dawn breaks, I stop at a point that leaves him breathless and yearning for more. And so the King spares my life for one more day, so that he might hear the rest of my dark tale.*

*As soon as I finish a story... I begin a new one... like the one that you, dear reader, have before you now.*

# Chapter One

"Girls! What have I told you about running around Uncle Ollie's house? You could step on a nail or knock over a can of paint. Plus, it's not polite to go crazy when you're a guest."

The girls stopped on a dime, then aimed angelic faces in his direction. "Sorry, Uncle Ollie," Lara said, her big, brown eyes on him. She poked her little sister, Anne, a wide-eyed imp, who piped up with, "We'll be good."

Ollie grinned. "You two are always good. Clearly your mom is confused."

At nine, Lara immediately burst out laughing, but the more literal seven-year-old frowned, then shook her head. "No, Uncle Ollie. We were being little pests."

He shot a glance toward their mother, Nikki. She tucked a lock of blond hair behind her ear, her sea-green eyes dancing as she struggled not to laugh. "You, my friend, are a bad influence."

"Hell, yeah," he said with a shrug. "Isn't that part of the Uncle job description?"

"It's definitely part of being an aunt," Jamie said from across the room. The three of them—Ollie, Jamie, and Nikki—had formed a tight triangle of friendship back in Texas, and those bonds had held strong over the years and the miles. They'd been tested, sure, but there were no two people he loved and trusted more in the world than Jamie and Nikki.

"Oh, come on, James," Nikki said. "Being an aunt has nothing to do with it. You've always been a bad influence."

"She has a point," Ollie said dryly, then pretended to cower under her glare. Whereas Nikki had a girl-next-door beauty that suggested innocence, Jamie was nothing short of wildly sexy with a definite hint of badassery, a fact she knew well. And which she'd used to her advantage on more than one occasion before she'd met her match in Ryan Hunter.

Now, she shrugged, then looked at the kids. "What can I say? Your mom and uncle know me well."

Lara giggled, but Anne asked, "Can we have some cookies now?"

"Yes, can we?" Lara chimed in.

The entourage had arrived with a dozen freshly baked chocolate chip cookies from Upper Crust, an amazing beachfront bakery near Nikki and Damien's Malibu house.

"I thought we were giving those to Uncle Ollie," Nikki said, making Lara roll her eyes.

"*Mommmy*. You know he'd just share with us anyway."

Anne nodded. "Uncle Ollie is very polite."

"Only one each. Daddy's taking us to dinner tonight. More than one means no dessert."

They raced toward the kitchen, their responses of *okay* and *thank you* drifting back to the adults.

"Anything in there that will send a couple of rambunctious kids to the ER?" Nikki asked.

"Actually, the kitchen's mostly done," Ollie said. "I still need to put the cabinet doors back on, but at least this way we'll see them if they decide to hide."

"Do you want us to hang out for a bit? I wouldn't be any help if you were laying tile, but I can attach a cabinet door."

"She says," Jamie retorted. "I won't believe her until I see it with my own eyes."

"Then it's going to stay a mystery," Ollie said. "I'm not putting you two to work. I'm just glad you were able to swing by." Nikki had called earlier to see if he wanted to join them for lunch, and when he'd said that he was tied up painting, they decided to come see the progress.

"You're doing an amazing job," Nikki said. "The front of the house looks great, and the entry hall is amazing. I love the tile."

"I wasn't sure about it," he admitted. "But Mom had Saltillo tile in the Highland Park house. Nostalgia," he added, then winced. "Sorry."

"Don't be," Nikki said. "I'm nostalgic for the time I spent at your house, too."

He knew she meant it, but he still wished he hadn't said anything. He adored his parents, and he'd loved growing up in the posh Dallas neighborhood. Being next door to Nikki had only made it better.

For her, though, those years had been torture. The visits to his house were rare moments when she was free of her abusive bitch of a mother.

"This part is looking great," Jamie said coming back from where she'd been peeking into one of the halls. "But you've still got your work cut out for you back there."

"Don't I know it."

"Why don't you hire someone to come in and get it finished? Jackson could recommend a zillion contractors," she added, referring to Nikki's brother-in-law, a world-renowned architect.

"Because he wants to do it himself," Nikki said. "I get that."

"Yeah," Jamie said with a shake of her head. "Not so much. But whatever floats your boat."

"Seriously, though," Nikki said, "put us to work. Or is getting out of your hair the most useful thing we can do?"

"Maybe we should open a dozen colors of paint and let the girls create abstract art." Jamie's eyes danced with amusement. "Actually, that sounds fun. I might just help them."

"Interesting, but no. I think I'll forgo the abstract and stick with solid cream walls in this room," Ollie said. "Except for that one." He gestured to the wall to his left, perpendicular to the balcony door. "I was thinking of painting it that shade of blue," he said, indicating the one swath of color he'd spread as a test.

"I like that," Nikki said. "It's like the blue you see on a gas flame."

"Exactly." He knew she'd get it. "And it matches the blue flecks in the hearth tile."

She glanced around the room. "This place is actually livable. You've come a long way."

"Um, hello?" Jamie chimed in. "Did you not hear me? Nothing down that hall is even close to ready."

"Nothing on the two lower levels, either," Ollie said. "Except my bedroom and most of the en-suite bath."

"Kitchen, living, bedroom." Nikki counted the rooms off with her fingers. "That's all you need right now."

"Exactly," Ollie said, with more than a little pride. He'd bought the place a few years ago when he'd made the move back to Los Angeles to join the FBI full-time after a stint in Manhattan as an attorney. Located in the hills above Universal Studios, the place had been in terrible shape, which was why he'd gotten it for a song. For the last few years, it had sat empty, the improvements coming slowly as he had time.

"I'm almost completely moved in now. And it's a huge relief. Especially since the drive from Marina del Rey to downtown is a nightmare with all the construction."

"What's Jackson going to do with the houseboat?" Jamie asked.

"I'm not sure." The architect had lived on the houseboat when he'd first moved to LA, but now he had a house in the Palisades with his family. When Ollie had moved back, Jackson had offered Ollie the use of it, which was fabulous while he was renovating, but now that Ollie was no longer renting it, he had no idea what Jackson had planned. "I'm just glad this place is finally fixed-up enough that I can move in."

Jamie made a face as she pulled a hair-tie out of the pocket of her jeans and tugged her mass of dark hair up and into a messy knot. "The place is fabulous, no doubt. And I'm terribly excited about your three rooms. But did you forget about air-conditioning? Because it's suddenly stifling in here."

"Yeah," he said with a grimace. "I'm having issues with the AC. It has a mind of its own."

"I guess so." As she spoke, she lifted her shirt and start fanning herself, coming pretty damn close to flashing him.

"You want to be careful before this turns into a peep show…"

She waved his words away. "Not anything you haven't seen before."

"And I'm pretty sure Ryan doesn't want me to see it again," he countered as he went to open the huge sliding glass door to the balcony and the incredible view of the San Fernando Valley and Universal Studios below.

Her husband, Ryan, knew about their ill-advised tryst a decade or so ago. And thankfully that was long behind them. Even so, it was an awkward memory. They'd had fun, sure. A few rounds of guilt-ridden, confusing, sweaty fun. But sleeping with Jamie had been a mistake. And even though they could joke about it now, it wasn't something he liked to think about. Especially not now that he was single and, frankly, more than a little confused about what he wanted.

No, about *who* he wanted.

His body warmed in a way that was pleasant, but also perplexing, and he was grateful for the cool breeze.

The truth was, he'd been confused back then with Jamie, too. Apparently, he made bad choices when he was confused. But he was in his mid-thirties now, dammit. He didn't have time to be befuddled by life and relationships.

Besides, it was damned exhausting.

He dragged his fingers through his hair. He was wearing it short again, and somehow the habit was less satisfying than when it had been long. Then again, the habit wasn't going to help anything. But talking to his friends might.

He just needed to suck it up and start the conversation.

As if taking himself literally, he drew in a breath. "Um, so, how about

I grab a bottle of whiskey and snag some of the cookies for us?"

He saw the way Jamie and Nikki exchanged glances. They weren't fools; undoubtedly they realized he had something on his mind. For that matter, they were such good friends, they could all practically read each other's minds. Or they'd once been able to. Right now, he doubted they had a clue as to what he wanted to tell them.

All he knew was that it was time.

"Cookies and whiskey?" Jamie said. "You don't have to ask me twice."

"Great." He glanced around the empty living room. He had furniture being delivered in a week. Right then, there were some metal folding chairs and a card table. "Maybe we take an extra chair onto the balcony?" There was a small outdoor settee out there already, but it was only big enough for two.

Jamie's brow furrowed. "Did Jackson check it out for you? I don't want that big slab of concrete to snap off while I'm sitting on it and send me hurling to my death on the roof of the neighbor below you."

"Damn," he retorted. "Now you've taken all the fun out of it."

Jamie just tilted her head and stared him down.

"Two Jackson Steele thumbs-up," he assured her as Nikki—ever efficient—returned from the kitchen with the cookie box, a roll of paper towels, and a bottle of Basil Hayden.

"Are we just slugging?" Jamie asked.

That time, it was Nikki who stared Jamie down. "Hands full. Go grab some cups, would you?"

"I've got it," Ollie said. "I want to tell the girls they can watch something on my bed if they want to. The television's installed and everything. No satellite yet, but I can get all the streamers."

"And that's why he's the favorite uncle," Jamie said as Ollie headed into the kitchen. "I need to tell Ryan to step up his game. After all…"

He missed the rest of her words as by then, he'd rounded the corner into the kitchen and had been immediately accosted by the sound of squealing girls. A sound that only became louder when he offered them television time.

He grabbed three glasses, then like the Pied Piper led the girls out of the kitchen and into the living area, intending to cross the space to the balcony. Instead, he stopped short. Because there was Trevor Barone, looking every inch his Italian roots, with his dark hair and dark eyes. He even had on a black T-shirt and black jeans. He was lean, but muscular, and right then, Ollie was thinking about him far too much.

He tried to stop, but his mind was already spinning. The truth was, Trevor reminded him of Cary Grant from *To Catch a Thief*, one of his favorite old movies. He had an elegance about him that Ollie found—well, actually he found it sexy. And that, of course, was what he needed to tell his friends. What he'd probably be doing right now, if Trevor hadn't blindsided him.

Then again, when hadn't Trevor blindsided him? The first time he'd met the man, Ollie's mouth had gone dry, and he'd spent the rest of the weekend wondering where this new Ollie had come from.

*Definitely blindsided.*

And now here was his walking, talking weakness, standing in his living room holding a pizza box in the entryway as he chatted with Nikki and Jamie.

"Trevor!" Lara called, then ran to him. He squatted down, then put the pizza on the ground as he gathered the girls in his arms. Damien tended to have the team at Stark Security over to the Malibu house when a large case wrapped, and because of that, Trevor had known the girls for years.

That, in fact, was how they'd first met. Just casually by the bar, and Ollie had felt a sensual punch to the gut. It faded, sure, and they'd chatted. It had been fine. But later that night Ollie'd been unable to get the man out of his head. And not just in a *there's a guy I could grab a beer with* kind of way. More like the XXX-rated variety.

Which was more than a little disconcerting in light of Ollie's theretofore caveman understanding of his sexuality: Him straight guy. Woman's breasts nice. Women soft. Sex with them nice.

With Trevor, though, Ollie had somehow missed a very important memo.

Now, Trevor was crouched down, one girl in the curve of each arm for a hug. "You two are looking adorable. And getting so big."

Watching him, something flipped in Ollie's gut, and his mouth was suddenly dry. A moment passed, then another, then he realized he was standing there like an idiot, and forced himself to keep walking. "Hey," he said, hoping his voice sounded normal. "Good to see you, man."

Trevor stood, then took a step forward, a smile teasing at the corner of his wide mouth. His defined jaw boasted a hint of stubble, and his ears stuck out just a bit, which Ollie thought was just too damned endearing.

And that was the trouble. He'd been thinking about this man far too much. A man now standing in his home in jeans that were both well-worn and fitted enough to accent the fact that this was a guy in seriously good shape.

"I was down on Ventura Boulevard, so I thought I'd bring you dinner and see how it's coming." He glanced around. "Looking good. Need help?"

"What? Oh, no, I—"

"We're going to cut out before you rope us and the girls into helping, too," Jamie said, then smiled sweetly. Which, considering it was Jamie, was never a good thing. "Errands," she added with a shudder.

"So many errands," Nikki said, then hurried closer to give him a hug. Maybe it was just his imagination, but it seemed a little tighter than usual, as if she was silently giving him support.

She pulled away, then called for the girls to follow. "Don't let him work you too hard," she said to Trevor. And then after a flurry of hugs from the kids and an order from Jamie to call her later, they disappeared.

He was alone with Trevor.

*He was alone with Trevor.*

He shoved his free hand into the front pocket of his jeans.

"Sorry," Trevor said.

"What? Sorry? Why?"

He nodded toward the glasses in Ollie's hand, then at the cookies and whiskey that Nikki had left on the ledge in front of the fireplace. "I think I interrupted family time."

"What? No. They were just in the neighborhood. Stopped by to see my progress."

"Just like me."

"Yeah," Ollie said. "Just like you."

*Except not. Really, really not.*

"Except not really," Trevor said, and it was a good thing Ollie hadn't yet poured and sipped the whiskey, because right then, he would have spit it out from shock.

"Not? What do you mean, *not?*" And when had his voice gotten high and squeaky? He was losing it. He might as well just melt into his brand-new teak flooring and be done with it.

If Trevor noticed that Ollie had turned into a blithering mess, he didn't show it. He simply moved closer and took the glasses from Ollie, leaving Ollie with nothing left to clutch like a security blanket. "Just that I came to help, not simply to check out how much you've done."

He crossed to the hearth and put the glasses down next to where Nikki had left the whiskey. "What do you say?" He opened the bottle without waiting for Ollie to reply, then poured them each a shot. "Shall we pick up a couple of brushes and knock out this wall. It's going to look incredible in that blue."

He returned, handed Ollie his glass, and remained standing just a little too close for comfort.

Ollie took a sip, then stepped back, hoping to find the air breathable again.

"Right." He cleared his throat, trying to remember Trevor's last words. "I mean, yeah. I think the color's going to really make the room." He wanted to head-thwap himself, if only to knock his thoughts back into alignment and banish any errant fantasies to the deep, dark recesses of his mind where they belonged.

*Except why did they belong there? Why couldn't those fantasies be front and center?*

Because Trevor was a friend. And Ollie didn't want to take a false step and screw up a friendship.

A statement that was one hundred percent true. And not the real reason at all.

The truth was, Ollie was pretty damn certain that Trevor wanted more than just friendship. They may have started out that way—even despite Ollie's disconcerting initial jolt of attraction—but then Ollie noticed that Trev had started touching him from time to time. Nothing major. A hand on the shoulder as they waited in line for a movie. A tap on the arm while they chatted at a bar. Casual touches. Subtle.

At first, Ollie only noticed the touches. Then he'd craved them.

Dammit, he truly had wanted—no, *did want*—more.

And the only reason he wasn't going for it was that he was a hypocritical, fucking coward.

"—just go?"

"I'm sorry, what?"

The corner of Trev's mouth curved up, revealing a small dimple. "I said that if you'd rather, I can just go. You seem a little distracted. Did I catch you at a bad time?"

"No, it's okay." Ollie gave himself a swift mental kick in the ass. "I am distracted. The air-conditioner," he lied. "I was thinking about something Jamie said right before you got here. That I need to get that thing fixed before we're into full-on summer."

"In that case, I'll take a look at it later. Might have some ideas. And in the meantime, we can paint or we can eat the pizza while it's hot. Sausage and pineapple pizza plus whiskey? Does it get better than that?"

Ollie made a show of crouching in front of the box, lifting the lid, and making a face. "I'm thinking it does."

"Not a fan of pineapple pizza?"

"Hey, I'm not one to turn down a free pizza. And I'll try anything once."

The moment the words were out of his mouth, he wished he could call them back. But Trevor didn't jump on the opening, and for that, Ollie was grateful. "Let's blow off painting," he finally said. "I'm done with work for the day. But I can get behind pizza on the balcony."

Trevor grinned. "Folks, we have a winner."

# Chapter Two

While Ollie carted the whiskey, glasses, and paper towels outside, Trevor grabbed the pizza, then followed Ollie onto the balcony. There was only a small outdoor bench—metal with a cushioned seat and back—and he put the pizza down in the middle, then looked around.

"Got a folding chair or something we can use as a table?"

"Yes. Good idea. Hold on." Ollie put the glasses and other things on the bench, too, then disappeared into the house.

As soon as Trevor was alone, he exhaled, his entire body relaxing. He was being a selfish ass, and he knew he shouldn't have come by, especially not without calling first.

He had a solid friendship going with Ollie, and he didn't want to ruin it because he was acting like a schoolboy who didn't know how to handle a crush.

But he did have a crush. And if he didn't dial it back, he was going to ruin a friendship he truly valued.

Ollie was straight. Or if he wasn't, he wanted to be. He'd had a lifelong crush on Nikki Stark, which everyone knew. Trevor was pretty sure he'd slept with Jamie at some point. And he knew that Ollie had been engaged to a woman named Courtney.

Straight. The guy was straight.

Even if there was a thread of queer in Ollie's blood, he'd spent a lifetime either ignoring or suppressing it. The man was a good friend. That was all.

Trevor needed to get that through his thick head. And the sooner he did, the better.

Too bad his libido kept ignoring that very sound advice. Ollie had rung all his bells since the first time he'd met the attorney-turned-FBI-agent when their paths crossed back when poor Anne had been kidnapped. But their friendship had truly solidified not long ago at a party they'd both attended in honor of Jamie's first starring role in *Intercontinental*.

By then, he'd been crushing hard, and it had only gotten more intense when Ollie had pulled him in to help on an FBI money laundering sting at the Mercury Club, a gay strip bar in LA. Trevor had wormed his way in as an actual stripper, and Ollie had posed as a customer. The operation had lasted a couple of weeks, and Trevor'd had plenty of time to watch Ollie in the audience. To see what he thought was a spark of interest in his friend's eyes.

Maybe he'd been imagining it, but he didn't think so. And that spark had lit a fire under his own desires, raising the heat from slow burn to full-on boil.

But real or not, Trevor knew damn well that Ollie was fighting it.

Honestly, crushing on a straight guy was a pain in the ass.

He could tell himself that forever, but it didn't stop the tightening in his chest or the sparks of awareness that shot through him when Ollie returned carrying the folding chair. He was wearing paint-splattered jeans and a similarly stained white tee that did nothing to hide the fact that the guy was in great shape. He'd heard Jamie tease him for being skinny, but Trevor didn't see it. Maybe before Trevor knew him, but if so, the guy had filled out. Ollie had always looked pretty damn delicious to him, with solid pecs, strong arms, and a tight ass that he really wanted to grab.

*And so much for that whole dialing it back thing.*

Mostly, he liked Ollie's face. The way he smiled. The expressiveness of his eyes. Those long lashes.

*Fuck.* Seriously, just *fuck*.

"Here?" Ollie said, indicating the folding chair, and it took two solid seconds for Trevor to shift gears and figure out what he was talking about.

"As a table. Right. Perfect."

Ollie nodded, apparently unaware that he was stirring Trevor up from nothing more than merely existing, then he opened the chair and centered it in front of the bench.

A few minutes later they were settled, drinks in the built-in cupholders, and the pizza on the chair in front of them. Their legs were stretched out, their feet propped up on the low concrete barrier into which the posts for the railing were set. Now they were kicked back, eating and talking and laughing.

It was good. Definitely good. Hell, right then he didn't care if he never touched the man. Or, more honestly, he cared. He cared a whole lot more than he wished he did.

But he'd deal.

What choice did he have?

* * * *

"This is a stellar location," Trevor said, then took a sip of whiskey and sighed. "I could sit here all day looking at the view."

"I have to work hard not to," Ollie admitted, feeling a rush of pleasure simply from the fact that Trevor liked his place. "One of these days I'm going to talk to Jackson about extending the balcony. Right now, it's too narrow."

As if to illustrate the point, he gestured from where they sat on the bench to where their feet were propped at the balcony's barrier.

"I love that idea," Trevor said. "And it shouldn't be too hard for a guy with Jackson's skills." He leaned forward, his shirt untucking at the back to reveal a strip of tanned skin.

A strip that Ollie noticed, dammit.

"Sorry," Ollie said, only then realizing that Trevor had been talking. "I missed that."

"I said I assume you own the hillside land. Worst case, he could set a post or something, but I bet he could just extend it with a few trusses attached to the house itself."

"Were you an architect in another life?"

"Nah, but I like working with my hands."

"Right." Ollie cleared his throat, deliberately not thinking about Trevor's hands. "Leah mentioned that once." Leah was Trevor's roommate and another agent at Stark Security.

"My hands?" Trevor's brows rose. "I'm flattered she noticed."

Ollie rolled his eyes. "That you'd fixed up a house."

"Yeah." There was a definite chill in his voice. "That I did."

"Sorry. Didn't mean to touch a nerve."

Trevor waved his hand, as if shooing away bad omens. "No, it's me. Not the fondest memories."

"Again, sorry."

For a moment, silence hung between them. Then Trevor reached for another slice of pizza. "It was with Greg. My ex. We'd been together for just over two years when the law finally changed and we got married."

"So fucked up that there had to be a change in the law in the first place. And now the bullshit of knowing that right might be taken away."

"No kidding." Trevor grimaced. "Then again, probably would have been easier if I'd never been able to marry the guy in the first place. Would've saved a lot of trouble on the backend."

"Don't even joke about that," Ollie snapped. "You loved him. You wanted to spend your life with him. It's absurd for anyone to say you can't, or that it's a lesser marriage than between a man and a woman."

"I know. Believe me, I agree. Stupid joke on my part. Marriage wasn't the problem. Marrying Greg was."

Ollie started to say that Trevor didn't have to tell him any of this; it was obviously a sore subject. But at the same time, he wanted to know. Maybe that made him an asshole, but he stayed silent, taking a sip of whiskey as Trevor continued.

"Anyway, first thing we did was buy a house. Nothing says marriage like community property, right?"

"So they say."

"Yeah, but what they don't mention is that when community property is divided, it's an expensive, stinking pain in the ass."

"You got divorced." He knew Trevor was single, so that was easy enough to figure out. "And I'm thinking it wasn't a congenial breakup."

"A thousand times no. It was a nightmare."

"What happened?"

"Things seemed fine for a while. I was working at Stark International doing security. He had a job doing film restoration. We had a yard, a garden, and a dog. I thought we were happy. We were sure as hell domestic. Two years later, he left me for someone else."

"Oh, man. I'm sorry. How did it happen? How did he meet him?"

"Him?" Trevor asked.

"They guy your husband left you for."

"They met online. And the pronoun would be *her*, actually. Turns out he started trolling dating apps about two months after we moved into the house. I found out because he left the app open on his computer the same day he called from work and asked me to forward something in one of his files."

"Oh, Trev. I'm so sorry." Ollie'd had his share of heartbreak, but nothing like that. Nothing both out of the blue and perplexing. "You had no idea he was interested in women?"

"I knew he was bi. We'd actually spent a lot of time talking about it. Or, in retrospect, he was just paying lip service. Told me he loved me, and that was all that mattered. I believed him. I never thought—"

He broke off with a shake of his head. "Anyway, that night, I confronted him when he got home. He told me he didn't want to be gay anymore." Trevor said the last part with finger-quotes. "How was I supposed to argue with that?"

"Sounds like you're better off without him."

"Damn right."

"But it still hurts." Ollie knew how that was. Courtney was better off without him for sure, but Ollie knew the on-again/off-again relationship he'd put her through had hurt her, and deeply. It had taken a long time for her to finally say that they were over. Thank god she'd had the guts to. He sure hadn't.

"Yeah, it hurt. I'd lost my mom about a month before, too. Single mom—I barely remember my dad. All I remember is him walking away from my fifth birthday party and never coming back. So, yeah, Mom was my whole world growing up. And then one day she was gone. I went into the garage to get the last of the groceries I'd picked up for her. When I left, she was telling me the plot of some soap she liked and making corn muffins to go with the chili she'd planned for dinner." He swallowed. "When I came back, she was dead on the kitchen floor. Aneurism. The EMTs said she wouldn't have felt a thing. I'm not sure I believe them."

"Trevor." Ollie put his hand on Trevor's arm. "I'm so sorry."

"It was hard. It still is. But it was different. She was older—she had me at forty-five—and we'd had some scares before, including a heart attack. So I'd faced it, you know? But then with Greg walking away..." He trailed off with a shake of his head. "That gutted me. I mean, shit, I even got sideswiped by panic attacks. Never expected that. Left me feeling like I wasn't the man I thought I was, you know?"

"Yeah," Ollie said. "I think I do. That must have been horrible."

Trevor nodded. "It was. But the worst was that it was Greg doing this. Hurting me. We'd meant everything to each other—or at least I believed that. Isn't that what marriage is? A statement of fidelity and togetherness?"

"I always thought so."

"Greg didn't. Either that or he missed the *you don't walk out on your husband* day of class." He waved the words away. "It shouldn't still matter. I've been over him a long time. And yet every time I think about it, I get worked up again. It's like the son-of-a-bitch cursed me."

"You still have the panic attacks?"

Trevor shook his head. "Managed to work through that. A bit of counseling. A lot of talking to myself. Greg's in the past. All of that is."

"Relationships are hard," Ollie said. "Especially when they're complicated."

Trevor turned, his eyes meeting Ollie's. "*When* they're complicated? Come on, Ollie, when aren't they?"

Ollie looked away, trying to ignore the uncomfortable zing of awareness that had shot all the way down to his cock. "You make a good point."

He reached to grab another piece of pizza, then jerked back when Trevor reached for his whiskey at the same time and their hands brushed. That yank back was embarrassing enough, but what was worse was the pizza landing cheese-and-pineapple side down on his crotch.

"Oh, hell," Trevor said, his fingers brushing Ollie's sauce and denim-covered package as he grabbed the errant slice. And in the process making Ollie practically leap out of his skin.

Immediately, Trevor drew his hand back, leaving the pizza where it fell as he leaned back, hands up as if in surrender. "Sorry, man. You know I wasn't trying—"

"No, I—"

"Just hang on," Trevor said, standing. "I'll get some paper towels."

Ollie opened his mouth to tell Trevor to wait—that he was the ass, not the other way around. But Trevor was already gone, and Ollie was left to peel the pizza off his pants while mentally kicking himself firmly in the ass for being such a, well, ass.

All too soon, Trevor was back with the paper towels, which he held out for Ollie to take while he remained standing, awkwardly shifting from foot to foot as Ollie started to mop up the cheese, tomato sauce, and pineapple bits.

"Right. Yeah, so, I should probably go," Trevor said.

"No, stay," Ollie said, the words tumbling out. "It's still early, and if you go, I'm stuck with not only pizza but cookies. I mean, how can you go without having at least one cookie with the whiskey?"

Trevor hesitated, his face a study of indecision. "It's a nice offer, but I think we both know I should get out of here. Maybe tomorrow we can talk. But—oh, hell. I really am sorry. I didn't mean to freak you out, and I wasn't—"

"Dammit, Trev, do you think I'm an idiot?" The words tumbled out without Ollie thinking about them, and he wasn't sure he could stop them even if he tried. "I didn't freak because I thought you were making a move. I freaked because I wanted you to."

# Chapter Three

"Oh." The word hung in the air as Trevor tried to decide what to make of that very bold—very unexpected—statement. "I'm not sure what to do with that," he admitted. Any other guy and he'd have him naked by now, but he'd never fallen for a straight guy before. Or mostly straight. Or a guy who thought of himself as straight.

"Do we have to do anything with it?"

"No," Trevor said, hoping he didn't sound disappointed. For months, he'd wanted exactly this—for Ollie to admit that there was an attraction between them. For him to acknowledge—to both himself and Trevor—that he wanted to do something about that.

"Right," Ollie continued. "It's just, you know, my mind is spinning." He waved his hand in the general vicinity of his head. "I mean, I'm not gay, so why would we?"

*Because you're curious. Because you're attracted to me. Because you want this as much as I do.*

He didn't say any of that. Instead, he just shrugged, flashed a cocky grin, and said, "I thought you were the guy who'd try anything once."

To his relief, the statement didn't freak Ollie out. On the contrary, he chuckled, his entire body seeming to release the tension that had been coming off him in waves. "So now you're a pineapple?" Ollie teased.

"Jerk," Trevor said, dropping back down onto the settee, then reaching for his glass and downing the rest of his whiskey in one swallow.

"Seriously," Ollie said, lifting his own glass and swirling the now-dwindling ice cube, "I—honestly, I don't know. But the bottom line is that you're a good friend. I don't want to screw that up. Did I?"

"Not even close. And for the record, I don't want to screw that up either."

"So we rewind?"

"Full stop rewind. Absolutely."

"All right. Good." He motioned to his pants. "I think I'm going to change into something less cheesy. I've got the TV set up in the other room. You up for watching a movie?"

Trevor leaned back, walking the tightrope of how much he could tease his friend under the current circumstances. "The other room? Didn't you tell me yesterday the only other finished rooms are the kitchen and your bedroom?"

"Yeah. It's in the bedroom. Streamers all ready to go."

"Come on, man. Are you trying to torture me?"

Ollie shot him a sideways grin that just about melted Trevor. "Damn right I am."

And just like that, the tension eased. "You can be such a prick McKee. I swear, I don't know why I keep you around."

Ollie shrugged, then shoved his hands in his pockets, his eyes not quite meeting Trevor's. "Maybe you like the way my ass looks in jeans."

Trevor forced himself not to laugh. "Well, yeah, there's that."

Ollie looked up, they shared a grin, and the last of the invisible band around Trevor's chest dissolved. It felt good to be back to normal.

"You mentioned something about a whiskey pairing with cookies," Trevor reminded him.

"Trust me. That's not something I'd forget. You take the bottle back. I'll go get some more ice and the cookies."

By the time they'd finished the first John Wick movie, they'd polished off two glasses of whiskey each and finished every cookie in the box.

"I think I'm in a sugar coma," Ollie said.

"I think I'm drunk," Trevor countered. They were sitting on the bed, propped up against Ollie's padded headboard, and as soon as he got home, Trevor was going to tell Leah the entire damn story just so he could get the props for making it through the afternoon without making a move on Ollie. A real one, not involving dropped pizza.

Then he was going into his bedroom, shutting the door, and jerking off. Because, damn, he was knotted up tight, and if he didn't release some of the tension, he would probably just explode in the night.

He shifted to see his friend more directly and say goodbye, and that's when he saw the chocolate on the corner of Ollie's mouth.

Never in the entire world had a tiny smear of chocolate looked so damned erotic, and despite the talk in the other room about not wanting to screw up their friendship, right then he wanted to throw all of that bullshit out the window and just go for it.

Wanted to lean in. To use the tip of his tongue to lick away the chocolate. And with the taste still lingering in his mouth, to press his lips over Ollie's until the other man opened to him. Until he surrendered. Because he would—Trevor was sure of that. All the talk about rewinding. About not screwing anything up. About Ollie not being gay.

It was all just so much noise.

Who gave a fuck if Ollie was gay or not? Whatever he was, he wanted Trevor. Of that, Trevor was certain. And god knew Trevor wanted Ollie.

And that tiny smudge of chocolate could make it all happen. It would be so easy. Just lean in and lick. And everything would change.

He could see it all play out in front of him. Ollie's gasp of surprise, his body going tense, only to loosen as Trevor deepened the kiss. As Ollie responded, tentatively at first, and then with gusto.

He'd take it slow, but he'd have him naked soon enough, and he'd trail kisses down Ollie's seriously ripped chest and abs until he reached his cock. And by then, he'd have Ollie so damned aroused he wouldn't protest. On the contrary, he'd beg.

That's what Trevor truly wanted. For Ollie to ask for it. Because once he did that, there were no more questions. Once he said *please*, all bets were off. And, yeah, it would change their friendship, but it wouldn't destroy it. Because even though he didn't know it yet, Ollie McKee was Trevor's. And soon enough, Trevor was going to claim what was his.

But not tonight.

As hard as it would be to leave, tonight he was going home. A little bit drunk, a lot horny, and very much alone.

Damned if he didn't have his work cut out for him. But it was his own fault. Because what was he thinking falling for a guy like Orlando McKee?

\* \* \* \*

Ollie had never been so relieved and so disappointed in his entire life. He should never have invited Trevor to his bedroom, because the whole damn time he was watching the movie he was thinking about *what if*.

If Trevor had quizzed him on *John Wick*, he wouldn't have had a clue. Except for the opening bit about the dog. After that, his head was somewhere else entirely.

As for right now, he ought to take a cold shower. But the truth was, he liked the way he felt, his body tingling, his cock on alert. They'd been playing at flirting, and damned if he wasn't aroused. So much that he'd almost let the whiskey take over. So much that he'd almost poured a few extra shots in the hope that Trevor would take advantage of the situation.

*So why didn't you?*

And wasn't that a hard question? And one that was getting harder to answer every time he asked it. And he'd been asking it for months. Ever since the Mercury case. Maybe even before.

But that case had solidified it. Being in that club with Trevor. Seeing him dance. Feeling that connection when Trevor focused on him. Probably just because he didn't want to focus on some anonymous face, but that wasn't what it had felt like. It had felt real. And more than once Ollie had caught himself thinking not about the money laundering scheme at the club but instead about what could happen in the small room when Ollie "paid" Trevor for his services.

A room that in reality they were using to pass information to each other, but which was intended by the club owners to be used for sex. And they'd been alone in there so many times, Trevor half-naked in a g-string, the room steamy in the faltering air-conditioning, and the memory of the way he'd gyrated on stage, his eyes glued to Ollie's playing in Technicolor in Ollie's brain.

Who was he kidding? For that matter, what was he hiding from? What was the worst that could happen? Losing the friendship?

He didn't buy that. Trevor knew Ollie's hesitations. If he freaked, Trevor would totally get it. And if the whole thing turned out to be one giant clusterfuck—haha—they'd just go back to their corners and redefine the relationship. Hadn't they proved on the balcony that they were more than capable of mature, grown-up communication?

Or maybe Ollie was freaking about the possibility of Nikki and Jamie and Damien and Ryan finding out. But so what? They wouldn't care. They loved him. Except maybe for Damien. And he couldn't imagine it impacting his job, but if it did, there were others. His parents might be surprised, but they loved him, too. All they wanted was for him to be happy.

And with every day that went by, Ollie was more and more convinced that at the core of it, his happiness and Trevor were inextricably intertwined.

That, of course, was why he'd almost protested when Trevor said that he ought to go home. But what would have been the point? He'd already told Trevor nothing was happening. So, what? Trevor would have crashed there, and Ollie would have spent the night wishing that his friend would slide over from his side of the bed so that Ollie could finally have a taste of what he'd been fantasizing about for months. Because despite all his justifying, Ollie wasn't ready to make the first move.

He should have, though. He should have leaned in with that whole pizza thing. Instead, he'd freaked.

Seriously, he was a fucking coward.

Or maybe he wasn't. Maybe Trevor wasn't what he wanted. Maybe this was just Ollie's psyche finally putting his relationship with Courtney to rest. Because even though it had been years since they totally pulled the plug, he hadn't dated anyone seriously since Courtney had told him she was done being a ping-pong ball in the off-again/on-again relationship Ollie had been steering.

Fair enough.

God knew, Ollie had been a shit. He liked Courtney. Hell, he loved her. But every time they got close to the wedding, he'd gotten cold feet. Because maybe he didn't love her enough. Maybe he didn't love her like *that*.

He couldn't blame her for finally tossing her hands up. She'd put up with him for longer than he deserved, and the way he'd bounced her around was at the very top of his list of lifelong regrets.

That, and not asking Trevor to stay.

Because, yeah, he wanted Trevor. And trying to convince himself otherwise was ridiculously, fucking stupid.

*Shit.*

The realization slammed through his head with such force that there was no denying it. Despite the talk on the balcony, once they'd settled down for the movie, that's what he'd expected. Maybe not sex, but something.

And, come on, let's be honest, he'd expected sex. Especially once he'd seen the way Trevor looked at him after the movie. Like Ollie was the secret surprise in the cereal box.

Still, he could hardly blame Trevor for going home, especially after how Ollie had freaked out about the damn pizza.

Ollie was an idiot. Not only that, but he was an unfair one, too. He owed Trevor the truth. Not the bullshit *we can be friends even though you're attracted to me* truth, but the real truth. The truth that Ollie was attracted right back. And he was just too confused or scared or unsure to do anything about it.

He'd spent his whole life thinking he was going to find a woman. Get married. Follow his parents' path. Then he met Trevor and everything shifted. How did he deal with that?

For that matter, could he trust that? What if the attraction was some sort of emotional and sexual rebound from the fiasco that was Courtney? He didn't want to hurt Trevor like he'd hurt her.

*And now you're really being arrogant, McKee. He's attracted to you, sure. But that doesn't mean wedding bells. You've slept with friends before. Look at Jamie. You're both fine. You even joke about it. Pursuing whatever this is with Trevor doesn't mean your whole life is going to flip. It doesn't mean a massive identity crisis. It just means you're hot for the guy. And, yeah, unexpected, but real. So why not pursue it? You can still be friends. You know you can.*

Maybe.

Or maybe he was justifying.

He was definitely thinking about it too much. Because right then he needed to go to sleep, but his head just kept spinning and he was so damn tired of these whirling thoughts filling his brain.

Apparently, identity crises were a pain in the butt.

With a sigh, he forced himself to just be still. To let sleep come to him. To think soothing thoughts. Like the fact that no matter what, he'd see Trevor tomorrow because Ollie had insisted he take an Uber home, which meant that Ollie had the keys to Trevor's BMW. He'd take it over in the morning, and in the light of day, all this angst would seem stupid and pointless.

Or, at least, he hoped it would.

# Chapter Four

Ollie was up at the crack of dawn, the thought of seeing Trevor again having not only prodded him awake, but also made him hurry though his morning routine.

Then he realized it was only eight on a Sunday morning, and probably a little too early to be dropping by. Which was why he spent the morning catching up on work emails and attaching cabinet doors in the kitchen.

He managed to occupy himself that way until ten, then showered, grabbed the keys he'd confiscated from Trevor, and headed to the front door, intending to put Trevor's BMW through its paces as he hauled ass toward Venice.

The moment he opened the door, he saw Cassidy Cunningham on the porch, her hand raised to ring the bell. They both jumped in surprise.

"Sorry. Didn't expect you to be right there," Cassidy said. Her hair was blue today with a few streaks of pink. It fell in waves just below her shoulders, and blended with the wildly colorful tattoo of an exotic bird that dominated her upper arm. "Do you have a sec or are you heading out?"

"Both," he said, holding the door open and gesturing for her to come in. "I was going out, but I'm not in a hurry. What's up?"

"I come bearing gifts," she said, stepping over the threshold as she passed him a small, blue gift bag, tied with red twine. "I just opened a third franchise, this one in Long Beach, and the first two are raking in a nice little profit. Plus, I wanted to see how your place is coming along."

A tattoo artist, Cass had started her career with one successful parlor in Venice Beach, not far from where Trevor shared a condo with Leah. A few years ago, when Ollie was still practicing law, he'd helped her franchise the business. "You didn't have to do this," he said, holding up the bag.

"I know. But I wanted to. It's just a token," she added as he tugged off the ribbon and peered inside.

"A token? Cass, this is awesome." He pulled out the small, blue-green bowl with free-form sides that gave the impression of the sea in motion.

"I have a friend who does blown glass work. It's a thank you and a housewarming gift."

"I have the perfect place." He led her to the fireplace and put it at the center of the mantle. "It even matches the wall. Not yet," he added, pointing to the slash of blue. "But when I finish painting."

"It's coming along, though," she said. "The place is huge."

"It's not as big as it looks from the outside. The illusion of building on a hill with multiple stories. But it's got three bedrooms and an office, so a decent size."

"Just you living here?"

For one awkward moment, a vision of Trevor hanging out in the living area reading a magazine popped into his head. He felt his cheeks heat and hoped that Cass didn't notice. "Yeah. Just me."

"I miss working with you," she said as he started to lead her on the tour. "But Jeff is great. Do you still keep in touch?"

"Every now and then." Jeffery Slade had been a summer associate assigned to Ollie the year that Nikki had moved to Los Angeles. He'd accepted the offer to join Bender, Twain & McGuire after he finished law school, and he and Ollie had worked together for about a year before Ollie moved to the firm's New York office and, ultimately, left for the FBI. "He's a good guy. Really sharp."

He took her all the way down to the lowest level that had been designed as a den, but that he was using as office space, then they moved upward, treading over the decrepit flooring, then moving past his fully finished bedroom and bath to the still-in-disrepair guest rooms.

"It's going to be great," she told him when they'd come full circle to the living area.

"It will," he agreed, though the walk-through had only reiterated to him just how unfinished and empty the house still was.

Once again, Trevor filled his head.

Once again, he pushed the thoughts away.

He cleared his throat. "So how are things with you and Siobhan?"

She made a face, and he winced.

"Sorry. Touchy subject? I thought you two were back together."

"Apparently that depends on Siobhan's mood and whether Mars is in retrograde." There was a harshness to her voice, and she waved a hand, as if pushing her thoughts away. "We're done for good. Honestly, I think she's Ollie and I'm Courtney."

He grimaced. "On again, off again?"

"Sorry, dude, but yeah. We were even engaged like you and Courtney were. And now we're permanently off. I don't care if she comes back naked on a barge bearing boxes of chocolate, I'm not going through that again."

"What happened?" The truth was, he'd never been certain why he'd put poor Courtney through so much. They enjoyed each other, laughed all the time, the sex was good, and they never lacked for conversation. Basically, she was perfect for him, and he'd asked her to marry him. Because that was what people did.

Except every time it got down to the wire, he choked. He'd push the wedding date, or he'd actually break up with her, though they inevitably got back together. And then, finally, Courtney'd had enough. She walked, and it had ripped him to shreds.

Except he still wasn't sure if he'd been devastated from losing the woman he loved or if he hadn't truly loved her, and the fact that he'd been an asshole to keep her dangling for years was what had twisted his gut.

*Bullshit, McKee.*

He knew the answer. He hadn't loved her. Not like that, anyway. But she'd been safe and familiar. She'd been exactly what a man in his position was supposed to have. And so, he'd grabbed hold, held tight, and kept her trapped for too long.

God, he'd been a shit.

"I'm sorry," he said, both to Cass and to the ghost of Courtney.

"Thanks, but it's okay," Cass said. "Siobhan and I had some good times, and I think she's great. But she couldn't get past her dad's reaction to her being with a woman. So now I've locked the door tight. My heart can only take so much, right? I mean, in the end, you have to figure out who you want to be with."

*Yeah. You damn sure did.* "And who do you want to be with?"

"Haven't found her yet. But when I do, I'll know." Her eyes narrowed. "Are we just catching up, or is there something you want to talk about?"

He shook his head. "No. Nothing. Just thinking about what a shit I was to Courtney."

"You're definitely not winning any awards over that relationship."

"Yeah, I fucked up."

"At least you know it. But the hard truth is that she wasn't your lobster. We just need to find our lobsters."

She wasn't wrong. But what if he'd already found the damn lobster, but was too scared to hold on?

\* \* \* \*

A few hours later, Ollie shifted from foot to foot as he stood outside Trevor's condo, working up the nerve to ring the bell. He considered simply leaving a note saying that he'd left the BMW in the building's garage. But then there was the question of the keys.

And the fact that he was being a total coward.

*Just do it.*

He did, and he could hear the echo of the chime through the closed door. What seemed like an eternity passed, then he heard the click of the lock, and he held his breath as the door opened, then let it out again when he saw who was standing on the other side of the threshold.

*Leah.*

"Hey," he said. "I figured you'd be at work today."

It was an idiotic thing to say, primarily because it screamed subtext: *I was hoping to be alone with Trevor.*

"Switched with Mario. What's up?" She leaned casually against the doorjamb, looking for all the world like a woman without a single clue why he was there.

He cleared his throat.

She lifted an eyebrow.

He passed her the key. "I brought Trev's Beemer over. It's in the garage."

"Cool. I'll let him know."

"Is he here? I was hoping to talk to him, too."

"Were you?"

The tension slipped out of his body, replaced by irritation. "What the fuck, Leah? Why the attitude?"

Her brows rose almost to her bangs, a style she'd switched to recently, with the rest of her hair brushing her shoulders. The look suited her, even when she was clearly irritated. "You're really asking me that?"

"Yeah. I'm standing here in the hallway, and I'm asking you that."

She blew out a noisy breath. "Trevor's out for a jog. Just give him a call later."

"Dammit, Leah, I—"

"For god's sake, Ollie, are you truly that dense? You're making him crazy."

"What do you mean?"

"Oh, come on. He's totally hot for you. You've got a major boner for him. Just go for it, already. Fuck him and see if you like it. Or if you just can't deal and that's never going to happen, then tell him so. Then you two can slide back into the friend zone, but that is not where you are now."

"Wait, wait. Hold on. We talked about that yesterday. We said we were rewinding."

"Oh, please." Her voice practically dripped with exasperation, and she stood back, holding the door open for him to enter.

He hesitated, but then sucked it up and stepped into the danger zone.

"So you're in third grade now?" she continued, closing the door behind him. He heard the whirr of the door's autolock underscoring her words. "You want to explain to me how you just snap your fingers and make all that go away? Did that work for you? You're happily swimming in the *just friends* vibe now? Is the water warm?"

Ollie pressed two fingers to the bridge of his nose. She was right. Rewind? Not even possible. He sighed. "You're kind of a pain in the ass, you know."

"I get that a lot. I'm protective of my friends, and he's at the top of the list. You're high up, too. If the situation were flipped, he'd be the one I was lecturing. God knows I've called him out enough for being an asshole."

"But today I'm the asshole."

"Oh, yeah. Big time." She crossed her arms over her chest, then leaned against the wall in the entry area. "Except you're not. Not really. You're just confused. So screw your head on straight and make good choices, okay?"

Ollie opened his mouth to speak, then shut it again.

"What?"

"You're a good friend. To Trevor and to me."

She grinned. "Love you, too." She cocked her head toward the living area. "Want coffee while you wait?"

Everything that had tightened inside him since she'd started ragging on him relaxed. "Yeah. That would be—"

He didn't finish the thought because he heard the distinctive beep of the code being entered into the front door's keypad lock.

"And that's my cue," Leah said, wiggling her fingers as she scooted out of the entryway. "Catch you later. And good luck," she added with a wink.

Ollie watched her go, then turned back in time to see the door open and Trevor stop short. "Ollie. I didn't know you were here."

He'd obviously been on a long run. A small towel hung around his neck, and his skin glistened. A plain white tee was plastered to his chest, highlighting his pecs. A tiny bead of sweat trickled down his temple, and Ollie had to fight the almost overwhelming urge to lick it away.

*Rewind, indeed.*

"I, uh, brought your car back. It's in the garage."

"Great. Thanks." He shifted his weight from one foot to another, drawing Ollie's attention to the damp running shorts that left very little to the imagination—and at the same time had his imagination firing in ways he'd never before experienced.

Ollie forced his attention back to Trevor's face as something soft but demanding fluttered in his chest.

Trevor tilted his head to one side, his brow furrowing. "So, do you want to hang? Or do you need a ride back to your place?"

"Actually, a ride would be great." He could hear his pulse pounding in his ears, so loud it drowned almost everything else out. Everything except his nerves. "But first there's something I meant to give you last night."

"Yeah?" He pulled the small towel from around his shoulders and mopped his face. "I'm intrigued."

"Me, too," Ollie said. And before he could talk himself out of it, he took two long steps forward, slid his fingers into Trevor's damp hair to cup his head, then pulled him close and kissed him.

# Chapter Five

God, it felt like heaven.

Trevor's hair brushing his fingers, Trevor's lips firm against his own. Ollie could hear his pulse pounding in his ears, and he was so lost in a haze of desire that it drowned out everything else, including the reality that Trevor wasn't kissing him back.

*Trevor wasn't kissing him back.*

A frisson of ice-cold terror shot through Ollie. Fear that he'd completely miscalculated. That Trevor truly did want to just rewind back to friends. And now Ollie had gone and set them up for ruin all over again.

But that thought faded as quickly as it had come because in the space of a heartbeat, Trevor went from rigid ice to bone-melting heat. His lips parted, and his tongue teased a low moan from Ollie, then a gasp as the kiss became deeper. Wilder.

Their mouths melded together in a passionate kiss that left them both panting for air. Trevor tasted like toothpaste, sweet and minty, and as they moved together in perfect harmony all other thoughts faded away from Ollie's mind except for one—this moment was perfection.

And then it got better.

Trevor took control. His hands cupped Ollie's ass, and he pressed his hips against him in an unmistakable way, letting Ollie know exactly just how much he wanted him. His hard cock was pressed tightly into the crevice between them, and the heat of Trevor's body sent a shiver of sensual longing through Ollie.

*He wanted this.*

He wanted Trevor. Every touch, every caress, every kiss. He wanted it all, would eagerly submit to whatever decadent pleasure Trevor demanded. Never once had he experienced the depth of longing he felt right now. As if he had no purpose other than this. As if he'd die if

Trevor stopped touching him, kissing him.

Trevor's kiss was a drug, and Ollie was definitely addicted. "More," he demanded when Trevor pulled back infinitesimally, terrified that Trevor was going to stop touching him.

"Hell, yes," Trevor said, the heat in his voice intoxicating. Then without warning, he spun them around so that Ollie's back was against the door, and all Ollie wanted to do was to melt. To be consumed. He was hard as steel, his skin tingling, and never in his life could he recall feeling so turned on.

"Trevor, oh, god, Trevor. I—" He cut off his words, not sure what he'd intended to say other than to beg for more.

But then Trevor pulled back, his brow furrowed. "Are you—"

"Don't you dare stop," Ollie growled, then cut off Trevor's delighted laugh by pulling him back and claiming his mouth again.

Another kiss, long and deep, and this time when Trevor pulled away, he gave Ollie a long, teasing look that sent a shimmer of anticipation racing up his spine.

Trevor's lips brushed the corner of Ollie's mouth as he kissed along Ollie's neck, gradually making his way to his earlobes. His hot breath tickled Ollie's skin, but it was his whispered words that drove Ollie over the edge.

"Do you know how long I've waited to taste you? Do you have any idea how much I crave you? How much I want your cock in my mouth. How hard I'm going to make you come?"

Ollie trembled with anticipation, his cock harder that it had ever been. He wanted everything Trevor promised, and he wanted to turn it around, too. To take charge himself. To taste this man. To touch him, explore every delicious inch of him.

Why had he wasted so much time being nervous? Feeling awkward? This was perfection. Exactly what he'd been craving even though he'd never realized it. Here, in this man's arms, he felt for the first time that he was whole.

With no small regret, he drew a breath, then eased back to meet Trevor's eyes, now a mix of raging heat and a hint of confusion.

"Where's your room?"

A slow smile eased across Trevor's face. "Follow me."

Trevor took his hand, then dragged Ollie into his bedroom and pushed him onto the bed. Ollie landed on his back, legs bent at the end of the mattress. A vulnerable position. And damned if he didn't like it.

Trevor grinned before backing away long enough to kick the door shut. Then he slid between Ollie's legs and tugged Ollie's T-shirt up, planting light kisses all over his torso as Ollie groaned with pleasure. But instead of focusing on Ollie's abs, Trevor went straight for the fly of his jeans, and the brush of his hand against Ollie's cock was enough to send him spiraling into ecstasy.

"I want you in my mouth," Trevor murmured.

"Yes. God, yes, please."

Slowly, Trevor unbuttoned the fly, then tugged the zipper down. Ollie closed his eyes, craving the touch. Longing for the release. Over Ollie's briefs, Trevor's fingertip traced the length of his cock, the light touch easing Ollie closer and closer to the cliff that he wanted to tumble over, locked in Trevor's embrace, their bodies shattering together.

But then, without warning, the touch was gone.

Ollie opened his eyes, craving the sensation of his cock in Trevor's mouth, even as he was terrified that Trevor had changed his mind.

"I just finished a run," Trevor said from where he was standing between Ollie's spread legs. A devious tease flashed in his eyes. "Pretty damn sweaty."

"Not caring right now."

Trevor tilted his head, then slowly trailed his fingertips along Ollie's erect cock, sending waves of pleasure through Ollie's body. "I'm thinking a shower would be a good idea." His voice dropped to a whisper. "And I think you need to join me."

Ollie hesitated, his heart thudding as the reality of what was happening suddenly hit him with full force. He was in Trevor's bedroom. He was about to get naked with Trevor.

And unless he was severely misreading the situation, he was about to have sex with Trevor.

"Whoa," Trevor said, apparently watching Ollie's face closely. "You want to stop, we stop."

Ollie turned ice cold. "I don't want to stop," he shot back, the words so hard and fast that there was no way Trevor could misunderstand the depth of his desire.

"Oh, thank God." The shadow in Trevor's eyes faded, replaced with a teasing glint that Ollie found damn sexy.

"It's just—" Ollie began.

"What?" Trevor extended his hand, and Ollie took it, drawing courage from the touch.

"It's just that—I mean, you know that I've never ... I mean, I don't know what...." He trailed off with a shrug.

"Trust me, you'll know what to do." His grin spread wide. "And if you don't? You're a pretty smart guy. I think you can figure it out."

\* \* \* \*

Trevor tugged on Ollie's hand to help him to his feet, not quite able to believe that after craving this man for so long he finally had him in his bed. He stared into Ollie's eyes and could practically taste the anticipation and desire radiating off him. *Ollie wanted him.*

He really wanted him.

With a grin, he pushed Ollie backwards, sending the man tumbling back onto the bed. "Screw the shower. We'll just need another when I'm done with you, anyway."

"Bold statement, Barone. Guess now you'll have to prove it to me."

"Twist my arm." Trevor wanted to scream with joy. Ollie might be nervous, but he wasn't letting it eat him up. He was flirting and playing and just being Ollie. And damned if that wasn't perfect.

He stepped closer. "Scoot back. All the way on the bed."

"Giving me orders?"

"Hell, yes."

"And if I don't follow them?"

"Oh, don't tease me." In one swift motion, he cupped Ollie's cock. "I could spend hours punishing you."

Immediately, he wanted to kick himself, hoping he hadn't gone too far—either physically or with the suggestion of the kind of games he desperately wanted to play.

But it wasn't awkwardness or trepidation he saw on Ollie's face. It was heat. And that—plus the way Ollie's cock had gone hard as steel under Trevor's touch—allayed his fears.

As soon as Ollie was all the way back with his head on the pillow, Trevor climbed on, too, his knees on either side of Ollie's waist, his hands on the mattress by Ollie's shoulders.

He bent forward, then brushed a soft kiss across Ollie's lips, his body tightening with satisfaction when Ollie opened to him, rising to meet Trevor's lips, his own hands clasping Trevor's head so as to deepen the kiss.

Hotter.

Harder.

Trevor moaned, his entire body tight and needy, desperate to touch this man all over. To tease him until he begged. To fuck him until they were both exhausted and spent, limp in each other's arms.

He remembered the first time he'd seen Ollie on Damien's pool deck. They hadn't spoken, but something within Trevor had sparked that day, and he'd craved this moment, even as he feared that he'd only ever have Ollie as a friend.

"What is it?"

"Just thinking." He sat back, then took the hem of Ollie's shirt and pulled it over his head. "Just thinking that I've wanted this since the first moment I saw you."

"I think I did, too, that first time we talked. I didn't realize it then—or I wouldn't let myself. But something about you grabbed hold of me."

"Something about *us*," Trevor corrected.

"Yeah," Ollie said. "Us."

"And the good news is that you're here. And right now, you're mine." *For always,* he thought as he ran his palms over Ollie's naked skin before lowering his mouth to tease his nipple even as he shifted his hips back, the better to feel Ollie's rock-hard cock teasing his ass.

"*Oh, fuck. Oh, man.*" Ollie's head arched back as Trevor teased and explored.

"Do you have any idea how much I've wanted this?" Trevor asked, tracing his fingertip along Ollie's jawline. "How many times I've fantasized about this moment?"

"Yeah," Ollie whispered. "Because I have too. I just didn't know—I was scared. So thanks for not pushing before I was ready."

"I won't say it was easy. You're walking, talking temptation, McKee. I don't think I ever believed we'd end up here. I looked at you and I saw Courtney. Hell, I saw Nikki. Jamie. And however many other women you had in your pocket."

Ollie groaned. "Does everyone at the SSA know about Jamie?"

Trevor chuckled. "Maybe not. I made it a mission to find out."

"And I've been over Nikki for ages. That was just a crush. A long one, but a crush. And you know it's over with Courtney."

"Yeah. I know." What he didn't say was that he knew Courtney was the one who'd ultimately ended it. It hadn't been Ollie's decision. That wasn't something he wanted to think about. But even as he tried to banish the thought, the memory of Greg popped into his head.

He'd told himself after the divorce that he'd never date another bi man again. But here he was, head over heels for this man in his bed. A man who'd fast become his best friend. Who now was becoming so much more.

"Trev?"

"Yeah?"

"As much as I love talking with you, do you think we could kill the conversation about my ex, and you can get back to kissing me?"

"Kissing? Babe, I plan to do so much more."

He eased forward again, his hands gliding up and over Ollie's taut chest until he was close enough to bend over and whisper. "I'm going to kiss you until you beg me for more. I'm going to suck your cock until you're right at the brink. And then I'm going to tease that sweet virgin ass before I fuck you until you scream my name."

As soon as he said it, he wished he could call back the words. He wanted it; damn right he did. But he didn't know if Ollie was ready for that. But then he heard Ollie's soft whisper—*Yes, oh, yes, please*—and he almost came right then.

"Trevor?"

"Yeah, babe?"

Ollie grinned. "We still haven't gotten back to the kissing part of tonight's entertainment."

Trevor laughed, then bent forward to rectify that oversight, but Ollie's palm against his chest stopped him.

"Thank you," Ollie said, and Trevor lifted a brow in question. "For not pushing before I was ready."

"Are you ready now?"

"I'm beyond ready."

They shared a grin. "Then it was worth the wait. Now shut up. Apparently, I'm supposed to kiss you."

Ollie opened his mouth as if to answer, but Trevor swooped in, silencing him with a kiss that started out gentle, but heated up fast. He gave up trying to prop himself up, and let Ollie bear his weight as they teased and tasted, tongues warring and hands roaming, as Trevor slid lower and lower, teasing kisses along Ollie's chest, watching as his abs tightened, then reveling in the way Ollie's body arched up, breaking the kiss when Trevor slid his hand into Ollie's briefs and stroked his cock.

"Oh, holy fuck." Ollie arched back, his fingers tightening in the bedding. "Don't stop. Don't you dare stop."

"Wouldn't dream of it," Trevor said, his circled hand keeping up a rhythm as his mouth worked its way down Ollie's body, desperate to taste him. To make him explode. To take Ollie to all the places he hadn't been before.

To once and truly make Ollie his.

He punctuated the thought by using his free hand to roughly yank Ollie's briefs down. Then he trailed kisses lower, reveling in the heady scent of musk and arousal.

"Don't stop. Please, don't stop."

Trevor didn't. Not even when the sound of the doorbell broke through their bubble. Not even when the ring repeated, a demanding buzz that barely penetrated the cloud of lust and desire that Trevor was floating on.

"Leah will get it," Ollie said. "Don't go," he added, as Trevor shifted toward the dresser.

"I'm not going anywhere. Just getting some lube." He slid up Ollie's body, then met his eyes. "You want that?"

Ollie didn't answer. Not with words, anyway. But the way he grabbed Trevor's face and drew him down for a hot, deep kiss was answer enough. And the answer made Trevor as hard as stone. He wanted that connection. Wanted to feel Ollie tight around him. Wanted to fist Ollie's cock while he pounded his own inside of him, until both of them came together.

And never once had he truly believed he'd ever get to live that fantasy.

"You're incredible," he whispered, catching himself before he said *I love you*.

But he did. He had for months. He was certain of it. But he wasn't sure Ollie was ready to hear it.

"*This* is incredible," Ollie retorted. He took Trevor's chin, turned it so they were facing each other. "We're incredible."

He lifted his head for a kiss, but their lips didn't meet. Instead, they were interrupted by the screech of Ollie's phone.

"Fuck," Ollie snapped. "I silenced that."

But the words were barely out of his mouth before he was sitting up, pushing Trevor off him.

"What?"

"I did silence it. There's only one ring that comes through when it's in DND-mode."

Trevor sighed. "Go ahead, Agent McKee. You better answer it."

Ollie did, hitting the button to put it on speaker even as the doorbell rang again.

"McKee."

"It's Horowitz and Ryan Hunter. Answer the damn door, Agent McKee."

# Chapter Six

The team gathered at Damien's Malibu house, a huge structure that not only boasted plenty of space, but was also already well-equipped to run an operation as massive as a kidnapping. Mostly, because it had already done that before. First, when sweet little Anne had been kidnapped along with Bree, their nanny. Then later when Nikki had been snatched.

*Kidnapping.*

He still couldn't believe it. But Horowitz, Ryan, and Damien had tracked him down at Trevor's condo because Courtney had been kidnapped, and the ransom note had been addressed to Ollie's attention.

Normally, they'd be set up at that the local FBI field office, but Damien had stepped in, and Ollie was still grateful. "He's going to want to work 24/7," Damien had said to Horowitz as they'd stood in Trevor's living room. "We all know that. Let's let him do that someplace more comfortable than a field office or the SSA."

"I'd like that," Ollie had said, and once Damien had pointed out that the house was already rigged for all the equipment they could possibly need, Assistant Special Agent in Charge Andrew Horowitz had agreed.

Ryan Hunter, the man responsible for the day-to-day operations of the SSA—not to mention Jamie's husband—had also agreed. But he'd insisted that the operation be a joint mission between the FBI and the SSA. And that Trevor run the op.

"He worked Hostage & Rescue before coming over to Stark International, and he's worked more kidnappings than anyone at the SSA. Plus, Courtney's one of ours."

Horowitz had turned to Ollie. "Your call, Agent McKee."

"The SSA knows what they're doing," Ollie had said without hesitation. "And Trevor's the right man to lead the op."

"Then you have no argument from me," Horowitz responded, an

Oklahoma twang coloring his voice. "Your group has a solid reputation in the community. And since I'm good friends with Anderson Seagrave," he added, referring to the colonel who headed up the covert Sensitive Operations Command for the Pentagon, "I can also attest to your reputation underground. We'll provide whatever support you need." He'd grinned. "Reserving the right to step in if we deem it necessary."

"Understood," Ryan had said.

Ironically, the only hitch had come from Ollie himself. "But we don't set up at the house until we're sure that Bree's okay with it," he'd said, referring to the Starks' nanny. She'd been kidnapped along with Anne on that horrible day. "Those days were a nightmare for her, and not just because she'd been taken, too," he added, looking pointedly at Damien. "I don't want our set-up forcing her to relive it all again. She hesitates even slightly, we move operations back to the SSA."

Damien had held his eyes, then nodded. "You're absolutely right. Why don't you call her? I'm her employer. I don't want her to feel like she has to agree with me."

"Thanks." Ollie had relaxed a bit, then. He'd been expecting a battle. At least some back and forth. But Damien kept surprising him. Still not Numero Uno on Ollie's favorite person list, but he wasn't a total shit. And he was definitely good for Nikki, even though it had taken Ollie far too long to realize that.

Bree had agreed without question, and now the whole team had gathered at the house, including tech geniuses Mario and Denny, who were working with the FBI's electronics team to set up all the equipment in the first-floor open area.

"Basing the operation here was a good call," Ryan said, standing by the third-floor railing and looking down at the hustle and bustle two floors below. He turned to face Damien. "We've got two other matters in active status back at the office. Better to have a solo space where we can focus."

"Agreed," Damien said, then turned to Ollie, his eyes full of compassion. "How are you holding up?" he asked as Trevor joined the group.

Ollie forced himself not to reach for Trevor's hand. He'd just returned from the first floor and was now standing close enough that Ollie could smell his cologne. He wanted to lean in. He wanted Trevor to put his arm around his waist and tug him close, sharing his strength and offering support. Instead, there was nothing but air between them.

He swallowed, then shrugged, not able to find the words. "I'm worried. For that matter, I'm terrified. But we've got good people working this. Don't worry," he said, speaking to both Damien and Ryan. "I'm not going to be a liability. I know how to do my job, too."

"No one's worried about that, Ollie," Damien said, his voice as gentle as when he spoke to his kids. "And you're allowed to be scared. I learned that one the hard way."

*Yeah, he had.* "Sorry," Ollie said. "I wasn't thinking. You've had someone you love kidnapped, too. Hell of a fraternity."

"Isn't it just?"

Damien put a supportive hand on Ollie's shoulder, then tilted his head. "I'm going to go see if there's anything the folks downstairs need before the briefing. Nikki's out with Bree and the kids. They're hurrying back. I'm sure she'll find you as soon as she gets here."

"Actually, I'll walk with you. There's something I want to ask you." He gave Trevor a quick smile—wishing it could be a quick kiss—then fell in step with Damien.

"What's on your mind?" Damien asked, pausing in the third-floor kitchen area. Nikki had told him that Damien had originally intended it to be a workspace for caterers, with the real kitchen down on the first floor. Instead, it had become the hub for their family.

Ollie pinched the bridge of his nose. "I hate to ask, but I want all bases covered, and in the end we may have no choice but to pay the ransom. If things go south, we might not get it back again." He drew in a breath. "It's a big ask—three million—but it's Courtney."

The kidnapper had left a note in the front seat of Courtney's Toyota, along with her cell phone. Three million to be delivered by Ollie himself or else she died. The drop point, it said, would come later.

Ollie hesitated, catching a glimpse of Trevor walking by. Then he forced his mind back on task, wondering if there would ever come a time when he wasn't distracted by the man. "Anyway," he continued. "Will you put it up? I don't know if I'll ever be able to repay you, but—"

"Ollie," Stark said gently. "I know it hasn't always been smooth sailing between us, but at the very least, I thought you were smarter than that."

Ollie blinked, not sure if he'd just been insulted. "I'm only—"

"It will be here within the hour. Two bags. Unmarked bills. And you're a fool if you think I'd ever expect you to pay me back."

"But—"

"What I do with my money is my call. And as I'm rather fond of fucking my wife, I'd like to stay on her good side and not leave one of her best friends hanging."

He grinned as Ollie rolled his eyes. "Nice, Stark. Real nice."

"Nothing that was news to you," he retorted, and actually made Ollie laugh. That, of course, had been his intent.

"You're okay, Stark. I may deny I said that a year from now, but right now, you're definitely not the shit I used to think you were."

"And from you, my friend, that is high praise, indeed."

\* \* \* \*

He found Trevor in the thick of it, moving among his people with a confident demeanor that added the right energy to the room. It certainly helped Ollie's mood. This was a man who got things done.

He'd known that already, of course. Not only had he enjoyed a view from the sidelines once or twice when Trevor worked—or ran—various SSA operations, but after they became friends, Trevor would talk to him about assignments, and Ollie would do the same, at least as much as protocol allowed.

They'd bonded over their stories and, oddly, over a talent for charades. They'd attended a party together, had paired up, then kicked every other team's ass.

That might have been the night he'd fallen in love.

*Love.*

Holy shit, it truly was. And how fucking terrifying was that?

Except lately, it was becoming less terrifying. On the contrary, it had become downright appealing.

And, of course, he'd seen Trevor's skill in both managing and working a case when they'd gone in together for the Mercury money laundering operation. Ollie might have already fallen hard for Trevor by that time—not that he'd told a soul—but that was the operation where he realized it wasn't just mental.

He'd *wanted* Trevor. To touch. To kiss. And, yeah, to fuck.

He'd sat in the audience, pretending to be a drunk patron as he watched Trevor strip down to nothing but a g-string, and he'd gotten hard.

It had been mortifying. No, it had been terrifying.

*It had been electrifying.*

But after a few days, those emotions had been replaced by something else. Not lust, but need. His mind already knew he needed Trevor in his life as a friend. Now, his body and his heart wanted so much more.

The knowing helped. That certainty of what and who he wanted.

Even now, though, there was an unease. It wasn't because Trevor was a guy. Ollie could give a flying fuck who anyone slept with so long as they were of-age and consenting. No, what still sort of bothered Ollie wasn't that he wanted Trevor—and god how he wanted him—but that he was meeting an Ollie he'd never known before. And how had he made it all the way into his thirties without having any idea that he was attracted to men?

He didn't have a clue about that, but he told himself it didn't matter. Why should it? The only important thing was Trevor. And as he looked at Trevor standing at the front of the room, confident and in charge, he couldn't remember ever being with anyone who gave him quite the same gut punch. He'd fallen hard, but it hadn't been fast. And he'd left Trevor hanging for far too long.

Earlier, he'd shown him how he felt.

Tonight, he needed to tell him.

He saw the instant that Trevor noticed him in the room. He'd paused in his conversation with Denny, a lithe blonde who was one of the sharpest agents at the SSA and pretty much a savant with anything tech. Now, he looked up, met Ollie's eyes, and flashed a quick grin.

That was all it took for Ollie to feel his cock tighten. God, he was a goner.

Was he really ready for this? Ready for what he wanted?

He was.

They'd been dancing around this for ages, hadn't they? Friends? They were way more than friends. But the heart of their relationship had always been buried under the surface. Today, they'd finally pulled it to the top. And that was exactly where it needed to be. Especially now, when Ollie knew that he'd need all his strength to get through this ordeal—and Trevor's strength, too.

Courtney might not be the love of his life, but she was special to him. And he intended to do whatever it took to make sure she came home safe.

"Hey, McKee. How are you holding up?"

Ollie jumped, realizing that he'd gotten lost in his own thoughts, because the man standing in front of him was entirely out of context.

"Brax? What on earth are you doing here?" He'd become friends with Braxton Reed at the Academy, and then they'd both gone their separate ways.

"Transferred to LA last week," Brax said, dragging his fingers through his thick, blond hair, the kind that any surfer would be proud of. Except that Brax didn't surf. Born and bred in Denver, Brax would probably be hard-pressed to even identify an ocean.

"LA? You? The man who used to rave about his time on the slopes. You do know that LA is pretty much sea level, right?"

Brax shrugged. "What can I say? They made an offer I couldn't refuse, and I came running. Besides, there's Big Bear. Mt. Baldy. Mammoth. California's not totally lacking for skiing."

"Not totally," Ollie repeated. "But say again? An offer you couldn't refuse?"

"Today's my first day at Stark Security," his friend announced. "I'm sorry about the circumstances, man. But I'm glad to be helping. I like Courtney. She doesn't deserve this shit."

"No," Ollie agreed. "She doesn't." He shook his head, still slightly bewildered. "Damn, though, it's good to see you."

"You, too. Despite the circumstances."

Trevor joined them and for a moment, Ollie caught a hint of something both harsh and vulnerable in his expression. But then he was beside Ollie, and he flashed that ridiculously handsome smile at Brax.

"You two getting acquainted?"

"Re-acquainted," Brax corrected. "We were at the Academy together."

"Roommates?" Trevor asked, and Ollie thought he heard an odd sort of tension in Trevor's voice.

"Just friends. You roomed with Dustin, right? Where'd he land?"

"Not sure," Ollie said. "We lost track after he got married. I heard he quit the FBI. Apparently the job made his husband too nervous." He shook his head, scattering the memories. "Seriously, it's great that you're here. The SSA's a stellar operation. You'll enjoy working in the private sector."

"So far, so good. I'll keep you posted." He turned to Trevor. "Assignment?"

"Check in with Liam." Trevor pointed to Liam Foster, a tall Black man with military bearing.

"On it," he said, then turned his attention back to Ollie. "We'll catch up more later."

Trevor stepped closer as Brax headed away, then tilted his head, indicating that Ollie should walk with him.

"Update?" Ollie asked.

"Nothing yet. But everyone has their assignments. I have you set up at station seven."

"Got it," Ollie said, starting to turn back toward the work stations. First order of business was to get into her electronics and see if she'd had a stalker, someone she was seeing, anything suspicious. And, of course, getting into her condo and seeing if there was anything telling there.

Trevor's hand on his shoulder stopped him, then steered him into the back hallway. "So, Brax?" His voice was low. "Just a friend?"

"Probably my closest friend at the Academy. We went through a lot of shit together."

"Anything else? A crush?"

Ollie narrowed his eyes. "No. And that's not the issue right now."

"No," Trevor said. "It's not." He closed his eyes for a moment. "Sorry. This whole thing—us—has spun me a little. You, I imagine a lot. We didn't have time to, um, debrief."

"Pity," Ollie said. "I think I'd enjoy debriefing you."

Trevor grinned. "Very glad to hear that. Seriously, though. You okay? Not with the Courtney situation, but with—"

"Yeah," Ollie said, forcing himself not to reach out and brush Trevor's arm. "I'd say that on that side of things, I'm doing just fine." He took a step closer. "And yeah, maybe there was a crush. But I didn't know it at the time." He looked up to meet Trevor's eyes. "And I'm very, very over it."

Trevor nodded, that adorable smile tugging at his mouth. "Glad to hear it, Agent McKee. Now you should probably get back to work. We both should."

"Yeah," Ollie said, wishing he had the balls to step even closer and kiss him. "I guess we should."

# Chapter Seven

Hours later, Trevor watched as Ollie paced the third-floor kitchen, a cup of cold coffee in his hand as he talked aloud.

"She doesn't have money. She doesn't have power." He turned to look at Trevor, pain evident in his face. "Why take her for ransom? It doesn't make sense."

"She's a journalist, right?"

"Yeah, for the last few years. She used to be in marketing. Big corporate marketing. Traveled all over the place, and the job was driving her into the ground. She quit, then was living on her savings for about a year. I think it was about four years ago that she picked up the journalism gig."

"And you two kept in touch after you broke up?" He heard the hint of jealousy in his voice, and hoped that Ollie didn't pick up on it.

"Yeah. We're still friends. I thought she'd run far and fast from me after what I did, but she's got a good heart."

*But do you love her?*

He didn't ask it. Why would he? He already knew the answer. He'd overheard Ollie himself saying it to Damien: *You've had someone you love kidnapped, too.*

*Love.* Not loved. The present tense.

He shook himself. A woman had been kidnapped. What the fuck kind of asshole was he for dwelling on how Ollie felt about her?

With no small amount of effort, he forced himself to regroup, then turned his attention back to Ollie. "What about family money? Could that play into this?"

Ollie shook his head. "There used to be. But they hit hard times a few years ago. As far as I know, they're leveraged to the hilt. Probably beyond."

Trevor nodded, thinking. "The kidnapper might not know that."

"True enough. We'll work that angle."

"What kind of journalism? Investigative? Maybe she stumbled across something."

"No, nothing like that. Assignments for entertainment magazines, mostly. That kind of thing. Puff pieces." Ollie checked his watch. "I need to call her parents, but I'm going to wait another hour. They're on vacation in London, and I don't want to wake them up with this news."

He started pacing, shock and grief etched on that face Trevor had come to know so well.

"What a conversation that's going to be. Hey, it's the asshole who kicked around your daughter, and by the way, she's been kidnapped. Don't worry, the ransom is taken care of, but so far we don't know shit."

Trevor took a step toward him and held out his hand. Ollie didn't take it. Slowly, Trevor pulled his hand back. "We'll get answers," he promised.

"Yeah, but it doesn't feel like it right now."

"I know." He put his hand on Ollie's shoulder, and Ollie immediately shook it off and started pacing again.

Trevor sighed, frustrated and confused. "Come on, Ollie—*oh!* Fuck me," he said as he realized what they'd all been missing.

Ollie stopped pacing and turned to face him. "What?"

"We're too close. I'm off my game. You, too."

"Dammit, Trevor. What are you talking about?"

"This isn't about a ransom," Trevor said, watching as confusion played over Ollie's features. "It's not about money at all. Not at the core."

Ollie shook his head. "What are you talking about?"

"It's about you, McKee. The ransom note was addressed to you. Not to her parents. And it's no secret that you're in tight with Stark. Whoever did this had to know that you'd be pulled in right away."

Ollie went completely pale. "Me," he said. "The sick bastard took her to punish me."

\* \* \* \*

Within minutes, the team was assembled around the conference table, and Ollie was beating himself up for somehow being at the crux of this. He shot a quick glance toward Trevor, who met his eyes, then shook his head just slightly. The message was clear—this isn't your fault.

Short and to the point, and it made Ollie feel a tiny bit better, if for no other reason than knowing that there was someone who had his back.

Their eyes held another second, then Trevor turned his attention back to the table and nodded at ASAC Horowitz. "Can you take a look at Ollie's closed and cold cases?"

"Already on it," Horowitz said, holding up his phone.

"I'll call Charles," Ollie said, referring to his old boss in Los Angeles. "See if anything rings a bell from one of my old cases here. But off the top of my head, I've got nothing."

"And New York?"

"I'll call the office there, too, but it seems more likely this would have originated here."

"Agreed," Trevor said. "But no stone unturned." He held Ollie's eyes again. "Whatever it takes, we'll get her back."

That warmth in his belly was back, and Ollie nodded. "Yeah," he said. "We will."

"You need to examine your personal life too," Quince said, his British accent more pronounced since he'd just returned from a job in London and come straight to Stark's house. He was former MI6 and an ex-member of Deliverance, a now defunct organization that had operated vigilante style, but with the primary mission of protecting and rescuing kidnapped children. Liam had also been part of that group, and Ollie couldn't be happier they were both on the team.

"I have been," Ollie assured him. "Honestly, no one rings any bells."

"What about Courtney's boyfriend before you?" Denny asked.

Ollie shook his head, doubting that would lead anywhere. "She had one serious relationship before me, and he's married now. Courtney was even in their wedding. They're close friends—Courtney, Bill, and his wife. But I'll go see him. If she'd noticed someone watching her or was nervous about anything, she might have told him."

Ryan leaned forward, his elbows on the table. "Wouldn't she have told you? After all, you're with the FBI."

"She would. At least I think so. But no stone unturned, right?"

"Oh, we've got something." From the end of the table, Brax looked up. "A partial license plate."

*Thank God.*

It wasn't a resolution, but at least they were moving in the right direction.

"Hang on," Brax said, tapping keys on his laptop. "Mr. Stark, can you dim the lights?"

Damien moved to the panel and did, adding, "But it's Damien. Not

Mr. Stark. That goes for all of you."

"Roger that. Okay, look." He gestured toward the giant LED screen that had been set up for the team. Black at first, then the video feed came into view. "This is the parking lot in Studio City at Laurel and Ventura. The area we're looking at is right behind the Vons where her car was found after the 911 call was received."

Ollie's eyes were fixed on the screen. Someone—presumably the kidnapper—had put in a call to 911 just after midnight from a payphone outside of the grocery store, which was how the ransom note had been found in the first place.

"Here," Brax said, and a graphic of a yellow arrow appeared on screen, indicating little more than a shadow. Then the shadow moved, crossing the visual field and coming into dim focus to reveal Courtney.

Ollie closed his eyes, fighting a wince. He knew what was coming. And soon enough, it did. A dark figure approached as she was about to open the driver's side door. He got her from behind, his hand going over her mouth, and Courtney going limp in his arms.

"Chloroform?" The question came from Nikki, and he looked over to see that she'd joined them and was standing beside Damien, his arm around her shoulder.

"Very likely," Brax said. "Keep watching," he added as the perp dragged her out of frame.

"Well, shit," Ollie said.

"Hold on." Brax tapped some keys, the image shifted, and they had a view of another car as the kidnapper carried Courtney to a late model Honda, then shoved her into the trunk.

Ollie's gut twisted at the sight. "Tell me you got a plate."

"Only a partial," Brax said. "But we have footage of the Honda driving west through the lot, approaching her car. Still only a partial, but it tells us that our suspect entered off of Laurel Canyon about that time."

"When exactly?" Trevor asked.

"One-oh-four in the morning. No idea what she was doing at the grocery store that late."

"She wasn't," Ollie says. "It closes at ten. She must have been coming in from across the street. There's a little bar tucked away on Ventura Place. She goes there about once a week to meet a friend from college."

"There you have it," Trevor said. "Someone might have known that habit. Leah, you'll take point interviewing the bar staff."

"On it," she said, shooting Ollie a sympathetic smile.

Next, he assigned Mario the task of going deeper into her work. "Poke through her files. Read whatever she was currently working on. Maybe she was trying to get out of doing fluff pieces. Maybe she was working on something investigative that took a wrong turn. Denny, you know what you're doing."

"Trying to track the car by that partial."

"Got it in one."

"That's all good and well," Ollie said. "But it doesn't feel right. This won't be about some article she was writing. The note came to me specifically, but anyone watching her would know we haven't been close in years. Somehow, this is tied to my work."

"What we know," Trevor said, "is that we don't know anything for sure yet, and so we're covering all bases. You know the game, Ol."

"I do." He pinched the bridge of his nose.

"We'll get her back," Trevor said, his voice intimately soft. "And we're definitely playing the Ollie card. You need to be in deep with that. Going over any intel we get from the firm or the Feds. Letting us know if anything is missing."

"I know," Ollie said. "And I'm all over that. But first, I need to talk with her parents." He gestured at the table and Trevor nodded, clearly understanding him. Trevor would hand out the rest of the assignments while Ollie went to make the call.

It was nice, that silent communication. They'd had a rhythm going for a while now, just as friends. But it had definitely ramped up. And in the midst of a hellish day like today, that was at least one ray of sunshine.

\* \* \* \*

Ollie was fighting a low-grade headache when he walked into the third-floor kitchen and sat down at the table across from Nikki.

"They're devastated." He could still hear the sobs of Courtney's mother echoing in his head.

"I'm so sorry," she said, taking his hand.

"They're in Europe. Some business trip. I told them they should stay put for now. At least they'll have some distraction from the worry. I told them we'd contact them the moment we knew anything, but they were worried they wouldn't be able to get a flight that would get them here fast."

He stood up, then moved to the coffee machine and programmed a latte. "I told them that we'd take care of getting them home. That Damien would send one of his jets. I'm sorry. I should have asked first."

"Don't be ridiculous," she said. And just like that, he felt a little better. No matter what other shit he was dealing with, he knew that Nikki would always be his rock. And through her, even Damien.

"Did they have any ideas as to who could be behind it?" She asked as Damien walked into the room.

"The parents?" Damien asked.

Ollie nodded. "Just got off the call. And no. Nothing. As far as they know, she's got no enemies, there have been no new boyfriends, no angry old ones." He reached up and massaged the muscles in his neck. "The bottom line is it's because of me. It must be. Someone is doing this to punish me."

"Or just for the money," Nikki said.

"Nikki has a point," Damien said. "Courtney has a connection to us, and she's a lot easier to grab than Nikki or the kids. Especially now."

Ollie nodded slowly, seeing where they were going with this. "But people know you. They know you're generous. So it wouldn't be a bad gamble that you'd pay the ransom for your wife's best friend's ex-fiancée."

"Which doesn't help us at all," Nikki said. "If that's the case, it could be any psycho who reads gossip columns. And that doesn't narrow the field."

"No. It doesn't." Ollie rubbed his temples, feeling like they'd come full circle back to nothing, then grabbed his latte. As he did, Bree came into the room. "Sorry to interrupt. I just wanted to get a snack for the girls."

"No interruption," Nikki said. "This is your home, too."

Ollie had the impression Bree was going to say something else but then Damien said a soft, "Damn."

"Bad news?" Nikki asked.

"Nothing about the case. It's Ash," he said, referring to Ashton Stone, the adult son that Damien only recently learned even existed. "He was going to come in this weekend, but he had to cancel. Then again, considering all we have going on, it's probably just as well."

Beside him, Bree shifted and Ollie got a look at her face. There was an odd expression on it, something a little bit soft. It almost reminded him of how he'd felt about Trevor before he could do anything about it. Except on Bree's face, there was relief there, too. And he couldn't help but wonder what she was thinking.

# Chapter Eight

Trevor took a sip of the black coffee he'd just poured, then sighed with pleasure. The day had been whipping by, and he needed the buzz.

Leah reached around him to grab the pot from the Mr. Coffee they'd set up in the work area. It wasn't as high-tech as the machine on the third floor, but it brewed coffee, and as far as Trevor was concerned, that was good enough.

She poured a cup, then took a sip, her eyes on his face.

"What?"

She lifted a shoulder, then let it fall. "Just wondering how you're doing."

He was tempted to respond with a terse *fine*, but this was Leah, and she knew him better than anybody. "Honestly, it's rough." He leaned against the wall, suddenly feeling completely exhausted. "Ollie's broken up. And at the same time he seems to be avoiding me. I mean, I want to comfort him. Help him. But there's this gap."

"A gap?"

He shook his head as if trying to organize his thoughts. "We were in bed. I mean we'd finally leapt over the giant elephant in the room, but there's absolutely no indication that ever happened. We haven't even brushed fingers this morning."

"I get that. But under the circumstances..." She trailed off with a shrug.

"I know. But I want to be there for him. Hold his hand. Put my arm around him. He hasn't touched me once since we left the condo. As far as anyone else is concerned we're nothing more than friends and co-workers."

He could hear himself talking and felt like a total jerk. Of course there were bigger things to worry about. More than that, it shouldn't bother him. But it did. Especially since after so many years, the kidnapper had drawn Ollie in, as if he and Courtney were still intertwined.

"I guess the crux of it is I'm jealous. I'm jealous of a woman who's been kidnapped, and I hate myself for it."

"Would it help if I said that sounded pretty natural? And so long as it's not screwing with your head enough to keep you from leading this operation, I say cut yourself some slack."

"You're right. I know you are. And yet my mind keeps spinning." He set his coffee cup down and ran his palms over the stubble on his jaw and chin.

"You should tell me. Maybe letting some of it out will shut down the noise."

He hesitated, then shrugged. "Fine. I heard him talking to Damien. Basically the conversation boiled down to the fact that Ollie loves her."

Leah took a step closer, then took both his hands in hers. "He probably does," she said gently. "They were close for a long time. And love has a lot of permutations. Hell, I love you, even when you are being dense and emotionally overwrought."

Trevor smiled. He needed that.

"Seriously, I get what you're saying. But Ollie basically came out five minutes ago. So what were you expecting? For him to cry on your shoulder in front of everyone at the SSA? Did you think he'd hold your hand while we work?"

"No. Of course not." He frowned. "Honestly I don't know that I was expecting anything. I just..." He trailed off, then sighed. "I'm just afraid that this was an experimentation for him. And now he's got cold feet."

"Would that be the end of the world?"

He wanted to say no. There were other men out there. But instead he told her the truth. "I think it might. It broke me when Greg left, but he wasn't the one."

"And you think Ollie is."

"Yeah, I do. But that doesn't mean he sees it, too. Ultimately, it has to be up to him. And maybe he's already made that choice."

She squeezed his fingers. "Then let's hope he chose to be all in, but right now you have to focus, my friend. Whatever their relationship, whatever your relationship, he cares about her and you care about him." She squeezed his hand tighter. "Do your job, Barone. The rest will sort itself out."

"I guess it will." He managed a grin, then pulled her in for a sideways hug. "I knew there was a reason I kept you around."

"For the record, I think you two are a match. And we both know I'm rarely wrong."

"No," Trevor said, "you've got good instincts. Let's hope you're right on this one."

\* \* \* \*

Ollie stood on the third floor, looking down at the operations center on the first, his eyes on Trevor. The man was competent. Sexy. And damned if Ollie didn't want him. The realization had been a shock—but only in the sense that it hadn't been a shock at all. It had simply seemed *right*.

The miracle, of course, was that Trevor wanted him right back.

And yet here Ollie was—absolutely head over heels, not to mention desperate to finish what they'd started in Trevor's condo—and he still hadn't told his best friends. Before, he'd been an idiot not to share his growing feelings with them.

Now, digging in about his love life seemed crass. His attention—all of his attention—needed to be focused on Courtney. Finding her. Helping her. And not just because that was his job even if the kidnapper hadn't thrust him into the middle of this. No, the truth was that Courtney mattered to him. He loved her, no question about it.

He just didn't love her in a way that was romantic. Not anymore. It hadn't been for a long time. For that matter, it hadn't been even before they'd finally broken up, and it was all on him for dragging that out.

She was a friend, and he was grateful for that. Considering everything he'd put her through, she would have been justified to walk away and never look back.

But she hadn't. They weren't close anymore, but they were still friends, and he'd never forgive himself if she'd seen this coming—if she'd been in any way scared or uncomfortable—but hadn't reached out to him for help because of their past and the shitty way he'd treated her.

He drew in a long, deep breath, wishing he could talk to Trevor about that. About how he'd let down this woman who'd been so special to him. But how could he? Courtney was his ex, and he and Trevor were still navigating their way into what he hoped was a relationship and not just sex.

With a frown, he ordered his brain to settle. To quit showing him mental images of what they could be doing to her.

Of her terrified eyes.

Of her wrists bound with cable ties.

Of Trevor's delicious smile.

Ollie winced. *Yeah, he was a mess all right.*

He took a breath and forced his attention back on the buzz of activity two floors below. Jamie was there now, carrying a box of bakery goods that she dumped on the conference table. She headed for the stairs, then looked up and smiled when she saw him.

She started climbing, reaching the landing as Nikki came in from the kitchen.

*And wasn't that convenient?*

"Overseeing your domain?" Jamie asked him.

Ollie shook his head, then looked between the two of them, gathering his courage. "Can I talk to you two?"

Nikki and Jamie exchanged a glance. "Of course," Nikki said.

"Here?" Jamie asked.

Ollie considered. "How about the balcony?"

"Sounds good." Nikki led the way through the bedroom suite over to the balcony that had the most privacy. There was a chaise lounge and two chairs, and Ollie took one of the chairs while the women sat on the chaise facing him. "So what's up?" Jamie asked.

He started to speak, then froze.

Then he mentally kicked his own ass and ordered himself to tell them because it was the truth and they wouldn't care. They'd be happy for him.

"I slept with Trevor." The words fell out in a rush. "Or, more accurately, I was in the process of sleeping with Trevor when we found out about Courtney. Even with that horrible interruption, best time of my life."

He sat back, watching their faces as he waited for them to say something. When they didn't, he squirmed, cleared his throat, and went on. "I, um, I guess I'm falling for him. Actually, I think I've already fallen for him."

The two women exchanged looks, and as Ollie's stomach started twisting, they both broke out into grins. "About time," Nikki said.

"We've known for ages," Jamie said. "We weren't sure you did."

"You knew? That I was crushing on Trevor?"

"Oh, please. Have you seen the way you two are around each other? It's great. We like Trevor. I think he's perfect for you."

"And in the interest of full disclosure, Sylvia said she's always wondered if you were gay or bi," Nikki added, referring to Jackson's wife and Damien's former executive assistant. "And that was without even seeing you with Trevor."

"She did?" He shook his head, amused. "Always good to be the last one to your own party."

"But it feels good to finally be there, right?"

"Yeah. Yeah, it really does. I was keeping a secret from myself, and I don't even know why. How absurd is that?" He glanced from Jamie to Nikki. "And you two? You're okay with it?"

"Why wouldn't we be?"

Nikki raised an eyebrow. "Are you seriously asking that? Ollie, it's us. And what's the big deal? I'm happy for you. What about Trevor?"

"What do you mean? We've always known he's gay."

"Yeah. But I meant how does he feel about you—I'm guessing it's mutual?"

"It sure feels that way. And he says it is."

"That's perfect then." Nikki's smile was wide. "That's how it should be."

"It feels right. You two get that, don't you. With Damien and Ryan? It was the same, wasn't it?"

"Very much so," Nikki said as Jamie nodded and silently mouthed *oh, yeah*.

Nikki reached out for his hands, then tugged him over to the chaise. She tucked her head onto his shoulder. "I'm so happy for you."

"So Trevor's the first guy you've actually been with," Jamie began, "but what about that cute roomie you had when you were doing FBI training. Dustin, right? You mentioned him like three times when you were telling us your *How Ollie became James Bond* story a while back."

"You're a hoot," Ollie said, but he seriously thought about the question. "Nope, not really. I liked him as a friend, but nary a zing. But," he added, "I think it was during that time that I realized I was bi. I just didn't tell myself until after I met Trevor. But now I'm..."

He trailed off with a shake of his head.

"What?"

He waved a hand in dismissal. "It's nothing."

Nikki shifted to face him. "We need a little more to go on."

He looked out toward the ocean. For a moment, he just watched the waves crash in, feeling a bit like a piece of flotsam tossed about in the roiling surf.

"I don't know," he finally said. "What if that was it and we're done? What if he regrets it? I mean, we didn't even—you know—*do* anything. What with Horowitz pounding on the door. But, I don't know. What if he regrets it?"

Jamie's eyes widened. "Why would he?"

Ollie shrugged. He'd felt a distance since they'd been pulled to Stark's Malibu fortress. Maybe it was his imagination, but what if it wasn't?

"You're a dufus," Jamie said, after he managed to—poorly—articulate his thoughts.

"Um, hello? I thought this talk was all about supporting your best friend."

"Yeah, not so much," Jamie said. "This is the reality check conversation, not the support convo. In this chat, you tell us the truth, and we sling truth right back at you."

She leaned toward him. "So, here's the deal. You told us that you had the best time of your life with the guy, and that's without doing all the things. And, by the way, I'm not taking that whole *best* thing personally. But maybe that's the problem."

He furrowed his brow, trying desperately to translate Jamie Logic. But it was Nikki who voiced the question. "What the fuck, James? I haven't got a clue what you're trying to say."

Jamie rolled her eyes, then locked them on Ollie. "You two came straight here from being all hot and sweaty and fast on your way to Happyland, right?"

He shifted on the chaise, a little uncomfortable with this whole conversation, then reluctantly answered. "Yeah. I told you."

"And yet you've barely even looked at the guy since you got here."

The words were like a punch in the face. *It was true.* Whether from general insecurity, an inability to deal with his feelings, rampant confusion, or just generally being a prick, he'd barely even acknowledged Trevor over the last few hours.

He glanced at Nikki, who nodded.

He closed his eyes. "God, I'm a jerk."

"No," Nikki said, reaching for his hand, then squeezing his fingers. "Maybe a little, but cut yourself some slack. You're overwhelmed. You're dealing with Courtney's kidnapping and with, well, all of this. It's been like five seconds. But Courtney used to be your fiancée. You two have a complicated history. It makes sense you're confused, even standoffish. But from his side, that's gotta hurt."

"You've both been paying attention?" The idea was both baffling and completely unsurprising.

"Duh," Jamie chimed in. "And we were starting to wonder if maybe we were wrong about you two."

"I wish you'd talked to me before. I could have used an ear or two."

"That goes both ways," Nikki said.

"Touché." He grinned at both of them, realizing he felt lighter than he had since Horowitz had pounded on the door. "You know, you both spend way too much time thinking about my sex life."

"Is that all it is? Sex?" Nikki asked.

"No." It was the easiest answer in the world. "No, and I'll rip my own heart out if I've hurt him." He sighed, feeling a little bit like an idiot for being so twisted up. "This shouldn't be weird or awkward. Why can't people just love who they love?"

"Love?" Nikki asked.

Ollie shrugged. "I'm just making a point."

The women exchanged a knowing look. "It's sweet," Nikki said.

"And you fell in love with him long before you fucked him." Jamie grinned. "That's kind of rare within our trifecta."

The three of them exchanged glances, then burst out laughing. "I love y'all," Ollie said. "You know that, right?"

"Duh."

"And I love Trevor. Or, I think I do." He really did. The sex part might be new, but he'd been slowly falling for him for months. "Why am I getting so up into my head about this?"

"Because when you crossed the line toward sex, you shifted your reality." Nikki shrugged. "Made you face the fact that you weren't only attracted to women. You needed time to adjust. That's all. I mean, come on. That's normal."

"I guess. But why should it matter in the first place?"

"It shouldn't," Nikki said firmly. "It doesn't. And fuck anyone who tells you otherwise. But that doesn't mean that you don't need time to readjust. To see yourself through a different lens."

"You're right," Ollie said. "And I'll say it again. I love you two."

"Of course you do," Jamie said. "I mean, honestly. How could you not?"

Laughing, they headed back inside, only to freeze when Trevor came into view. He was standing in the third-floor open area not far from the painting of Nikki that Damien had paid a cool million for. And the moment Ollie caught sight of him, his heart started to do that fluttering thing that was so uniquely his reaction to Trevor.

"There you are. I was coming to tell you we're meeting downstairs in five."

"Sounds good," Ollie said, as the women magically disappeared, leaving the two of them alone.

"You okay?" Trevor took a step closer, his brow furrowing.

Ollie shook his head. "I'm not at the top of my game. And I owe you an apology."

He saw a muscle twitch in Trevor's cheek. "Do you? Why?"

"You don't have to pretend like I haven't been an ass." He reached out and took both Trevor's hands in his own. "I'm so sorry. You probably thought I was avoiding you. I swear I'm not."

Tension seemed to melt from Trevor's body. "Good to know." He drew in a breath, then exhaled, a smile warming his eyes. And in that moment, Ollie truly wanted to kick himself, because that's when he realized just how much he'd wounded this man he would never, *ever*, intentionally hurt.

"And, yeah, I may have spent some time wondering if you'd had second thoughts," Trevor admitted. "Fortunately, I have a kidnapping case to keep me busy." The corner of his mouth ticked up. "Sorry. Bad taste. It's just—"

"No," Ollie said emphatically. "You don't owe me an apology. This is on me. I guess I was parsing out the rules, maybe? Overthinking? Being an idiot?"

"Maybe a little of the latter," Trevor said with a laugh. "I guess it's a good thing you're so cute."

Relief flowed through him, as warm as sunshine. "I am, aren't I?"

They shared a smile, holding each other's eyes in a way that had Ollie wishing they could justify some down time. That, however, wasn't on the agenda just yet.

"So how are things going downstairs?" Ollie asked.

"We're making progress, but it's slow. Not unexpected, of course, and you know the drill. But you haven't lived it before." He frowned. "Sorry. Actually, I guess you have."

He was right about that. Ollie had come as soon as he'd learned about Anne's kidnapping. And, of course, he was around when Nikki was taken. "Yeah, I have."

"But this is different," Trevor said, something odd coloring his voice. "Because you love her."

"It changes things," Ollie agreed. "I mean, I probably shouldn't be working this case at all, but there's no way I'm walking now. Horowitz couldn't keep me away if he tried."

They were still holding hands, and Trevor gave Ollie's fingers a quick squeeze before releasing them. "No, you'd find a way to see this through even if he locked you in a cage. That's who you are."

"Is it? Or is it just because this one eats at me more?"

"It's personal," Trevor said firmly. "It's Courtney. Of course it eats at you more."

Ollie nodded, ridiculously grateful that Trevor understood. He glanced toward the stairs. "We should get back to it," he said, and together they descended, reaching the bottom just as Brax was calling for everyone's attention.

"Bree made out our room assignments," he said, gesturing to the nanny, whose long, dark hair was pulled back into a ponytail. "You want to take it away?"

"Me? Oh. Um, sure." Bree brushed a stray strand of hair out of her face. She was a mix of Cherokee and Jewish, with stunning features and huge brown eyes. She was also incredibly poised despite being tossed into the middle of what had to bring back hellish memories of when she'd been taken with Anne.

"You'll be sleeping in shifts, obviously," she began, "but even so, some of you are going to have to double-up. I'm going to go around the room and tell everybody where they're bunking." She glanced down, then looked around until her gaze landed on Ollie. "You know where you are," she said, referring to the room he habitually stayed in when he crashed at the Stark home. "Trevor, you'll be—"

"Trevor's with me," Ollie said, searching the group for a reaction, his stomach settling when he didn't find one.

"No problem." She pressed her pen against the clipboard. "Who has which shift?"

"We're working and sleeping the same shifts," Ollie clarified. "You can use the room for someone else during our awake shift."

Bree nodded, made a note. "Got it."

Trevor slid a hand around Ollie's waist, then leaned in to whisper. "Nice move, trapping me with you like that."

Ollie had to force himself not to laugh. "I'm sorry I was an ass."

"We've been over that. You weren't. Besides I like your ass."

He wouldn't laugh. "Work harder on the jokes, Barone."

"I'll get right on that."

After the room assignment, Trevor went to go get a status update from Denny and Mario. At the same time, Brax sidled over. "I thought so," he said casually. "You two look good together."

"Thanks, buddy. I think so too."

# Chapter Nine

Two hours later, the night shift was running the investigation, and Ollie and Trevor were on deck to get a few hours of sleep.

"I want to be back at it by six," Ollie said, once they were in the room, "and it's already midnight. That only gives us four or five hours of sleep."

"It's a good thing you're a Fed and not an accountant," Trevor said. "Your math skills suck."

"On the contrary," Ollie said, taking Trevor by the shoulders and pushing him to the door just as Trevor had done at the condo. "I can subtract just fine. And trust me when I say you're not going to sleep quite yet."

Trevor laughed. "No argument from me."

Ollie hesitated, then met Trevor's eyes and almost melted in the heat he saw reflected back. "I really am sorry."

Trevor shook his head. "Stop. No more apologies. We're good. Relationships are tricky things. They can really fuck some people up."

Ollie leaned in, brushing his lips over Trevor's ear. "Then it's a good thing we're so well-adjusted."

"Yeah," Trevor said, his voice going breathy in a way that made Ollie even harder. "A very good thing."

"Trev?"

"Yeah?"

Ollie pulled back enough to meet Trevor's eyes again. "I want to finish what we started."

Trevor's smile was slow and heart-meltingly sensual. "That is the second best thing I've heard all day."

Ollie brushed his lips over Trevor's perfect jawline. "Second?"

"You. Me. Sharing this room."

Ollie swallowed, then shrugged. "I was getting in my own way earlier."

"Yeah, you were." Trevor took Ollie's hand. "So long as you're sure now, we're all good."

"Oh, I'm sure."

Trevor's grin was pure mischief. "You know what they think is going on in here right now, don't you?"

Ollie waited for the tug of embarrassment that didn't come. With a grin, he kissed Trevor softly, his teeth tugging on Trev's bottom lip as he pulled away. "I know," he said. "How about we try to live up to their expectations?"

Trevor chuckled as he grabbed Ollie's ass, pulling him in close. "Agent McKee, I thought better of you. Live up to? Babe," he said, his voice low and husky, "we're going to exceed them."

"Yeah? Maybe you need to prove that to me."

"Maybe I will," Trev said, then surprised Ollie by moving one hand around to cup Ollie's cock through his jeans, making him go even harder and his knees turn weak.

"Maybe that's what I want," Ollie said, his voice rough.

"Yeah?" Mischief flashed in Trevor's eyes, and before Ollie could reply, Trevor tightened his grip down below, then silenced Ollie's moan by claiming Ollie's mouth with his own.

His lips slid over Ollie's, his tongue exploring Ollie's mouth in a way that made his cock grow even harder, until he was straining against both his jeans and Trevor's hand.

All reason faded, replaced only by the need to touch. To feel. To have.

Ollie's hands slid around Trevor's waist, then down, his fingers splaying over Trevor's khaki-clad ass. He pulled Trevor's body against his and rocked gently, his cock and Trevor's rubbing together through their clothes. Trev's mouth was hot and wet and so damn perfect, and Ollie wanted more. So much more.

More pressure.

More contact.

More skin.

More of everything.

He wanted it all. But mostly, he wanted it with Trevor.

"On the bed," Trevor said, easing them away from the door and to the looming king size bed.

He gave Ollie a little shove, and Ollie sat obediently, back straight and his head tilted just enough so that he could look into Trevor's licorice-black eyes.

"You're fucking gorgeous," he whispered, reveling in the other man's dark hair with just a hint of curl. Those thick eyebrows. And the mouth that was absolutely made for kissing.

He'd felt the punch the first time he'd seen him. And when they'd become friends, he'd fought that feeling for far too long. Now, he was going to finally experience what he'd been craving…and so foolishly denying himself.

"On your back," Trevor said, taking Ollie by the shoulders and moving that process along. Soon, Ollie had scooted up the mattress, and Trevor was straddling him, the pressure of his ass against Ollie's rock hard cock not only maddening, but also inspirational. Because right then, the only thing in Ollie's head was what he wanted to do to Trevor—and what he hoped Trevor would do to him.

Slowly, Trevor leaned over until the material of their shirts brushed together, sending a fresh new wave of sensation tickling all over his skin. "You're driving me crazy," he said, his voice coming out in a rough whisper.

"Good. That was my plan. Now, hush." He traced his fingertip over Ollie's lips, and Ollie groaned, growing harder by the second. "Oh, yeah," Trevor said, moving his hips just slightly and amping up the sensation.

"Trevor." Ollie grabbed his wrist, trapping the finger that was teasing his lower lip. "Not so fast. I don't want—I mean, I want it to last."

Trevor's eyes narrowed, then he bent forward and claimed Ollie's mouth with his own. A deep, slow kiss, then building with intensity, so wild and so passionate it was almost like fucking, and Ollie never, ever wanted it to end.

It did, of course, but from the gleam in Trevor's eyes, he had an even better follow-up planned. "I should drag you into the shower just to finish what we almost started at my place, but I can't wait. I want you now."

"Thank God," Ollie said, the words coming so fast and so intense that he realized he wasn't nervous at all—okay, maybe a little. Mostly, he just wanted this.

"Close your eyes," Trevor ordered, and when Ollie complied, he felt the tug of his shirt being untucked from his jeans. Then Trevor's nimble fingers unbuttoning it. In a moment, the sides of the shirt were pushed aside, and he felt the cool air against his overly heated skin.

He started to open his eyes, but heard Trevor's low growl of protest and kept them shut. Then Trevor's hands were on him, exploring and teasing, his fingers dancing over Ollie's stomach and chest, his lips brushing lightly over his nipples.

It was like being on fire, and dear God, he wanted to burn.

Then he felt Trevor's breath at his waistband, followed by Trevor's fingers slipping under. Teasing him just enough to suggest a promise of things to come.

Overwhelmed and painfully hard, Ollie kept his eyes closed, his head back, his neck arched, and told himself to just feel. To just float. To let Trevor take him to whatever heights he wanted, because right then, Ollie would follow him anywhere.

And then he was falling, slipping deep into a well of pleasure. The scent of Trevor. The touch of him. The only sound in the room was their breathing and the seductive scrape as Trevor tugged Ollie's zipper down, and, yeah, Ollie had to open his eyes.

Trevor noticed and flashed one wicked grin, then slid down the bed, taking Ollie's jeans with him. Ollie wiggled, helping to ease them down and onto the floor, then found himself in only the open shirt and boxer briefs that did nothing to hide his arousal.

"That's what I like," Trevor said. He was on his knees at the foot of the bed, and he slowly climbed back up, this time cupping Ollie through the thin material. "Close your eyes again."

"This is completely unfair," Ollie complained as he obeyed. "You're still dressed."

Trevor made a show of looking at himself, and then at Ollie. "Works for me," he said as he tugged Ollie's underwear down, releasing his cock. The sensation of the cool air against his heated skin made him suck in air even while he fought the urge to just out-and-out beg.

That's when he realized that Trevor was no longer touching him. He opened his eyes to see Trevor looking at him with a grin that seemed both mischievous and deeply erotic.

"Tell me," Trevor said, easing Ollie's briefs all the way off. "Tell me what you want."

"Trev…" Ollie shook his head. They hadn't talked about this. They hadn't negotiated a relationship. They'd only even kissed a few hours ago.

So how could Ollie know what he wanted?

*Except he did know. He'd known for a long time.*

Since the money laundering sting, for sure. And, if he was being honest, even before that.

*Charades.* When you got right down to it, Ollie had known the first time they teamed up to play charades. That was, what? Over a year ago?

Back when Trevor had invited him to Zelda's place, the woman who'd written *Intercontinental,* Jamie's first big movie.

Granted, someone had been trying to kill Zelda, so the group of Stark Security agents had been there for a reason. Even so, the night had been fun, and the game even more so. He and Trevor'd had a rhythm. There'd been an edge to it. And he'd spent the whole evening in a sensual haze that had both terrified and excited him.

"Where did you go?" Trevor was leaning over him, so that Trevor's shirt was brushing Ollie's now-bare and very awake cock.

"I'm right here," Ollie murmured as he reached up, then pulled Trevor's head down for a kiss that Trevor enthusiastically returned. It was hot and wild and everything that Ollie wanted.

*Except not quite everything.*

"Trev..." He could hear the need in his voice.

"I know," Trev said softly. "Me, too." He shifted position, then lightly licked the tip of Ollie's cock. Ollie groaned, the sound low and deep, and though he tried to squirm, Trevor's strong hands were on Ollie's hips, holding him firmly in place.

With a deliberate slowness that drove Ollie mad, Trev used his tongue to tease and lick and suck—never fully taking him in, but playing with him just enough to have Ollie fisting his hands in the sheets, half out of his mind with need, but not quite to the edge.

He couldn't remember ever being so turned on. It felt like heaven. It felt perfect. And even though he craved that explosive loss of control, right then he never wanted it to end.

"God, Trevor." His voice was raw, needy, and he tilted his head back, eyes closed. He was completely at this man's mercy, and Trevor didn't disappoint, every lick and every touch designed to push Ollie right to the edge.

*Game on, indeed.*

And then, *oh, yes,* Trevor drew his cock fully in, his warm mouth enveloping him, sucking him long and deep until Ollie was fighting to keep from exploding, simply for the pleasure of making this sensation last.

But there was no fighting the way the pleasure was building inside him, like the increasing pressure of an imminent explosion. He opened his eyes, needing to see. Then watched as Trevor sucked his cock, the sight making his insides twist with a delicious need more intense than he'd ever felt.

He wanted the explosion. The release. And then, damned if he didn't want Trevor in *his* mouth. At *his* mercy.

That was the thought that pushed him over the edge. That had heat flooding him. That had his entire being teetering on a precipice, fighting against the desire to go over and the longing to stay exactly like this, hyper-aroused with erotic pleasure enveloping him like the crackling of electricity.

But then Trevor's other hand slid under Ollie's balls, his fingers teasing Ollie's crack until his fingertip found his ass. Ollie arched back, groaning. The sensation was incredible, and when Trevor licked his fingertip then gently teased it inside Ollie's ass even as his tongue circled the head of Ollie's cock, Ollie knew he had to either pull back or go completely over.

"Wait." The word was barely a groan, but Trevor stopped immediately, lifting his head, his brow furrowed with worry. "No," Ollie said. "It's good. It's amazing." Wasn't *that* an understatement. "But you asked—you asked what I wanted." He bit his lower lip, feeling ridiculous for feeling nervous.

"So I did," Trevor said, his head tilted just slightly, as if Ollie was a puzzle.

"What you said yesterday." Ollie licked his lips and didn't quite meet Trevor's eyes. "That's what I want." His cheeks burned. Was he actually blushing?

"Yeah?" Trevor asked, then moved up Ollie's body. He took Ollie's chin in his hand, forcing Ollie to meet his eyes. "Tell me," he whispered. "I want to hear you say it."

Ollie's chest tightened, and his mouth went dry. "You said you were going to fuck me." He bit his lower lip, then exhaled. "Please, Trev. That's what I want. Not your fingers. I want to feel your cock inside me."

Trevor's eyes went dark with lust, and his slow, sexy smile made Ollie even harder. Hell, right then he wanted to bury himself inside Trevor as much as he wanted to submit.

*Soon.*

He wanted this first. To be claimed. To be owned.

And he'd wanted it for one hell of a long time.

"I did say that," Trevor said, with his ridiculously sexy grin.

"Yeah. You did." Ollie propped himself up on his elbows and shrugged out of his shirt, tossing it off the bed. Then he reached out for Trevor's waistband. "You're overdressed for the occasion."

"That's me. Always with the social *faux pas*."

"Very gauche," Ollie agreed, his heart pounding as he watched Trevor slide off the bed, then slowly strip. Pants first, then briefs, so that his cock poked at the tail of his shirt before Trevor pulled it over his head and tossed it aside, revealing that stunning sculpted body. He unbuttoned his jeans, then tugged them down over his hips. He wasn't wearing underwear, and that unexpected revelation sent a fresh shot of sensual awareness zinging through Ollie. An awareness that only increased when Trevor crawled onto the bed—and Ollie—then kissed him hard before whispering, "You want to be fucked, McKee?"

"God, yes."

"Roll over."

Ollie shook his head, and Trevor raised his brows. "I want to see you."

Trevor grinned. "Fair enough."

"So, what are—"

"Shut up," Trevor said, sliding up Ollie's body and taking care of that by closing his mouth over his in a slow, deep kiss that sent electricity zinging through his body only to collect in his painfully hard cock. When Trevor broke the kiss, he winked at Ollie, grabbed a pillow, and ordered Ollie to lift his ass.

Ollie complied, and Trevor slipped the pillow under Ollie's hips before rolling off the bed and opening the overnight bag he'd brought. "Lube," he said. "And a condom. I figured just in case."

"I like the way you think," Ollie said, then arched back and closed his eyes when Trevor's lubed fingers teased his ass, the sensation almost enough to make him come right then. He heard the familiar sound of the foil package being torn and opened his eyes in time to see Trevor rolling the condom on his very large, very erect cock. He swallowed, his ass constricting, but not with nerves. *With need.*

So much need that he wanted to scream for Trevor to hurry. He was drunk with anticipation, heady with lust. "Please." The word was so soft he was surprised Trevor even heard it, but he saw the way his mouth curved up and those eyes dipped to skim over Ollie's body.

And then he was there, on hands and knees on the bed, his body over Ollie's, his slick fingers teasing Ollie's crack, his entrance, even as his mouth claimed Ollie's in kiss that started out soft but got harder and deeper in time with the way that Trevor's fingers were teasing Ollie's rear.

His mind was spinning. Wanting.

*Everything.* He wanted it all. He wanted Trevor.

Hell, right then, Trevor was everything, and as far as Ollie was concerned, if he didn't have him right then, he might as well just give it up and die. "Please," he said again.

"Yeah," Trevor said, breaking the kiss as he answered, then trailing kisses back down until he was once again over Ollie, the tip of his cock right at Ollie's slick entrance, one hand on Ollie's hip and the other on Ollie's cock.

Ollie arched up, his body craving what Trevor was giving, then cried out at that first push, tight and painful in a way that, yeah, hurt so good.

"You okay?"

"Don't you dare stop," Ollie said, his voice raspy with need. "More. Slow, but more."

Trevor said nothing, but his eyes never left Ollie's, and soon he'd filled Ollie completely, and Ollie had no choice but to close his eyes, not because it hurt, but because the intimacy of this moment was too intense, too wonderful. And then when Trevor moved inside him ... oh, dear god, it felt like the universe was splitting apart. Like he was being bathed in starlight. He felt owned. Possessed. Loved.

And then when Trevor fisted his cock and stroked Ollie in time with his thrusts, he felt nothing but a mindless pleasure that was more intense than anything he'd felt before. "Trevor—Oh, god, Trevor, I'm—"

But that was all he could say, as the power of speech and thought completely left as his orgasm crashed through him like a wave, his body shaking with pleasure as he shouted out his release even as Trevor came inside him.

The sensations seemed to last forever, and then Trevor slowly withdrew, and Ollie was left panting and satisfied and still wanting more as Trev settled beside him after disposing of the condom. Ollie turned on his side, so that they were face to face, and Trevor's hand rested on Ollie's hip.

"Wow," Ollie said, then inched forward to brush a kiss across Ollie's lips.

Trevor chuckled. "I was going to ask if that was good, but I think you just answered."

"You know it was," Ollie said. "Either that or I deserve the award for best actor."

Trevor grinned, but there was something hesitant in his eyes.

"What?" Ollie asked, a small knot of worry fighting its way to the surface through the sea of lingering bliss.

Trevor shook his head, looking mildly embarrassed. "Your first time. I was just—just taking a quick inventory."

Ollie laughed. "You can take my inventory anytime." He rolled over until he was on top of Trevor, relishing the sensation. And the control.

"And no, it wasn't weird. I don't feel awkward. I have zero regrets." He frowned, then tilted his head. "No, I take it back. There's just one thing that's not right."

He saw the flicker of fear in the other man's eyes. "What's that?"

"That I haven't had my turn with you yet." He grinned, feeling deliciously in control. "I hope you weren't planning on drifting off to sleep right away."

Trevor laughed. "No," he said, his hands sliding up to cup Ollie's ass. "Sleep is the last thing on my mind."

# Chapter Ten

"I'm very glad to hear that," Ollie said, reveling in the power of now being the one in control. He shifted position so that he was straddling Trevor's waist. Then he scooted back until he felt the glorious pressure of Trevor's cock against his naked ass.

Trevor sucked in air, his whispered, "Oh, fuck, yeah," making Ollie even harder.

With a mischievous grin, Trevor reached for Ollie, his hand closing over Ollie's cock and giving him a little tug. "Up here," he ordered. "I'm not done tasting you."

"Oh, no. I'm in charge now." Ollie's voice felt raw, his body needy. His hands roamed over Trevor, wanting to feel everything. To taste everything.

"In charge?" Trevor's hands slid around Ollie's hips, then moved on to his ass. "I don't know," he continued with a tease in his voice. "I liked having you at my mercy."

As he spoke, Trevor used his fingers to tease Ollie's crack, the gentle caresses once again growing into a significantly less gentle need.

"Yeah?" Ollie's voice broke a bit as his entire body burned. "Trust me when I say I already am. Let's see what I can do about evening the score."

He eased forward, and while Trevor continued to tease, Ollie did the same, his fingers exploring Trevor's abs and chest.

He sat up slowly, his cock fully erect again. He met Trevor's eyes, then saw his gaze dip to Ollie's erection.

"I like the view."

"Me too," Ollie said, trailing his gaze over Trevor's face, then his chest, then those gloriously ripped abs before dipping down to Trevor's perfect cock.

He sucked in a breath as a fresh jolt of desire cut through him, and he shifted position until he was straddling Trev. Immediately, Trevor's fingers moved to stroke Ollie's cock. A featherlight touch, but it lit a fire. He arched back, fighting not to come again right then. He was walking a tightrope, wanting the explosion, but not wanting this to end.

Mostly, he wanted to take Trevor over. To know he had that power, too.

With a bit of regret, he pushed Trevor's fingers away. "Oh, no. This is my show. Enjoy your front row seat."

Trevor's laugh rumbled through Ollie's body as he leaned forward until his hands were brushing Trevor's nipples, then his lips were on his neck, his jawline, his mouth.

He tasted like sin and seduction and perfection, and Ollie thought that Trevor might be the best kisser in the world. Sweet and firm, with just the right amount of wetness and tongue, and all designed to drive Ollie absolutely wild. Especially when Trevor twined his fingers in Ollie's hair and drew him closer, deepening the kiss.

Ollie lost himself in it, melting into bliss as his hands trailed up to Trevor's shoulders then around to caress the back of his neck. His lips moved from Trevor's mouth down to his jaw, then further still until they reached Trevor's collarbone.

He sat up, trailing his hands over Trevor's extremely well-defined abs as he did so. "Someone works out."

"We hot shot security agents have to stay in shape."

"Nice for me."

"You're not in bad shape yourself," Trevor countered, his hands sliding over Ollie's bare thighs, his right one continuing on to circle Ollie's cock. Slowly, he started to stroke.

Ollie moaned, then closed his eyes, desperate to once again succumb to the sensation. But there was something he wanted more, and with one firm movement, he pushed himself back until he was straddling Trevor's thighs, his cock right there waiting for him to taste it.

He did. Slowly at first, his tongue teasing the steel shaft as he moved up to flick the lightest of licks over the glans. He closed his eyes, reveling in the taste of precum even as he forced himself to go slowly. To draw it out. To make Trevor as insane with lust as Ollie had been. Slowly, he teased with his tongue, then drew his cock in, wanting to take all of it. Wanting to make Trevor scream.

He opened his eyes to see Trevor arching up, his hips trying to thrust despite Ollie holding him firmly in place. This was his show, after all. His call on how to make Trevor burn.

"Yes," Trevor murmured. "Christ, Ollie, yes."

With Trevor's words and moans urging him on, he increased his pace, drawing him in deeper, teasing with his tongue. Doing everything that drove him wild and more, and damned if it wasn't working. He could feel the tension in Trevor's body. That moment when he was so close to sending him tumbling over.

He shifted position, straddling Trevor's torso now instead of his legs, his back to Trevor's face.

"God, yes," Trevor murmured, his hands cupping Ollie's ass as Ollie once again took Trevor's cock in his mouth. This time, though, it felt as though Trevor was running the show. Because although Ollie could feel the tension rising in Trevor—could practically feel the orgasm coming on himself—Trevor was driving Ollie just as crazy by teasing Ollie's ass. By whispering how much he'd loved fucking him there. That he couldn't wait to be inside him again.

The words were a potent aphrodisiac, and his mouth worked Trevor in time with the memory, rising and rising until he was right on the edge again, and it was in that moment that Trevor arched up, crying out Ollie's name as he emptied himself, making Ollie feel like a goddamn hero in the process.

"Wow," Trevor said. "Seriously, wow."

"I second that," Ollie murmured after he'd slid off and moved to snuggle close. They were lying face to face, and when Trevor reached up to stroke Ollie's cheek, it felt like the most romantic moment ever.

"I—" He stopped. What could he say? *Want you? Need you? Love you?* They were all true—all of them, he was certain of it—but he couldn't push the words out. Not now. Not yet.

Instead, he just smiled. "I feel wonderful."

"Me, too," Trevor said, but his eyes said more, and Ollie moved in even closer, his forehead pressed against Trevor's chest. His eyes were so heavy. He wanted to stay awake, to tell Trevor how much this night meant to him, but sleep was pulling him under. And the last thing he felt was the soft, gentle brush of Trevor's lips on his head.

\* \* \* \*

Sleep called to Trevor, but at the same time, it eluded him. How could he sleep now, after finally—finally—getting what he wanted?

Not sex, though that had been amazing.

No, what he'd wanted was Ollie's submission. His consent. His trust. *His love.*

For well over a year, he'd craved this man, but he'd never been entirely sure where Ollie stood. There was an attraction—that much was for damn sure. But was Ollie just curious? Was it just sex and attraction and having a good time?

Or was there more there?

He'd spent far too many nights praying that there was more, because Ollie was the first man since Greg who'd made him feel fully alive. Who'd planted thoughts of a future into his head. Of a relationship. Maybe marriage. Possibly kids.

And, yeah, he was probably getting ahead of himself. It was only sex after all.

Except was it?

It had felt like so much more. It had felt like a promise.

More than that, it had felt like love.

*And the moment you lay that on Ollie, you'll send him screaming for the hills.*

Trevor shut the thought down, the possibility that he could scare Ollie away was just too damn depressing. And what was he doing thinking depressing thoughts right now, anyway? He'd just shared the best sex of his life with the man who was also his best friend. That wasn't something to fret about; he should be celebrating. They'd crossed a line. They were moving forward.

So what if Ollie had only slept with women before? That meant nothing. Ollie wasn't Greg. Ollie was a thousand miles away from the man Greg had been. A man who'd cheated, not only in marriage but in his own representation of himself. He'd specifically told Trevor he had no interest in women anymore. And even if he did, there was no way he'd break his vows.

And yet he'd broken them so easily.

With a sigh, Trevor moved closer to Ollie, his arm going around his waist. As he did, Ollie shifted, too, so that their bodies were spooned together.

"You're thinking too loud."

Ollie's whispered words startled Trevor into laughter. "I thought you were asleep."

"Mostly. I like the feel of you. Soaking it all in before I fade to black. No time for a repeat performance when we wake up. We'll be on point downstairs. I'm making the most of the memory."

Something worrisome tugged at his gut. That sounded like a one-off.

He swallowed. "Memories are good."

"Damn right," Ollie said, his voice thin with sleep.

And as Ollie drifted off again, Trevor fought down an emotion that felt remarkably like panic. Because he wanted more than just one memory with Ollie. He wanted a lifetime of memories.

Most of all, he wanted the man himself.

# Chapter Eleven

Trevor woke with a groan, the blare of the hideous alarm he'd set on his iPhone enough to make him want to hurl the thing across the room. He didn't; instead, he grabbed it, then stabbed blindly at the screen until the squawking stopped.

Then he flopped back, enjoying the blissful silence.

That, however, lasted only a minute, because as soon as he closed his eyes and tried to fall back asleep, he realized what had been bugging him—Ollie.

He wasn't in bed.

Frowning, Trevor sat up, then looked around the still-dark room. The curtains were closed, but it wasn't even six. The sun was still pushing itself up over the horizon.

The room had an attached bath, and Trevor got out of bed and walked naked in that direction, assuming Ollie would be there. But the door was wide open, and there was no sign of him.

*Okay…*

For a moment, Trevor felt a stab of fear. Had Ollie regretted last night? Had he found himself lying awake, trying to wrap his head around what they'd done? And, ultimately, had he decided that it wasn't for him.

*Get a grip, Barone.*

He wanted to kick his own ass. He knew he was a projecting Greg onto the situation. And now he was getting all up in his head, like a high school freshman with his first crush. He was an adult, dammit. More than that, he was a trained observer. He could parse out a scene by studying it, and frankly this scene didn't require much study at all.

It was morning. Ollie was gone. So, for that matter, were the clothes Ollie had been wearing last night. All of which added up to the certainty that Ollie had gotten dressed and left the room.

Not exactly the most mind-blowing bit of detective work, but at least he wasn't spinning wild tales of Ollie sneaking out the bedroom window with a blue-eyed blonde whose big tits had won out over Trevor's cock.

With a frustrated groan, he shook his head. He truly was losing it, and all because he'd fallen fast. But had it been too fast? Or was it like Goldilocks and the timing had been just right?

And like hell it was fast. They'd been dancing around this for over a year now.

He shook his head, forcing the swarm of thoughts to stop spinning.

He started toward the door, remembered that clothes would be a stellar idea, then slid back into the pants and Henley he'd been wearing. Sometime today, they'd need to grab some extra clothes and toiletries.

With the possibility of that joint excursion filling his thoughts, he headed out of the room, almost bumping into Brax.

"So where are we?" he asked. "Anything new in the night?"

Brax shook his head. "We're pretty much right where we were. A long way from nowhere, but unfortunately in the wrong direction."

"In other words, we've got nothing."

"Got it in one." He hooked his thumb toward the room Trevor had just come from. "You're clear, right? Apparently that's my crash pad."

"It's all yours. I was asleep when Ollie stepped out, but I assume he has everything he needs."

"Yeah, when he settled in downstairs, he said he couldn't sleep. Not surprised considering it's Courtney. I mean, no matter what's between them today, those two have a long history. He's got to be sick about this."

*Of course he was.* Ollie was broken up about Courtney, and Trevor was being a jerk for not even thinking that Ollie wouldn't be able to sleep. That of course he'd head straight down to the operations center.

He frowned; he was distracted and off his game, and he couldn't afford to be. *Courtney* couldn't afford him to be. Because they were going to find her. For her sake, and for Ollie's.

"I'm heading down now to get reports from the overnight crew and check in with everyone coming on shift. There's coffee, I hope."

"Gallons," Brax promised. "And cinnamon rolls."

"Who do I have to kiss to make sure those keep coming?"

"The pastry fairy?" He nodded toward the bedroom. "See you on the flip side—or you'll wake me if something pops?"

"You know it."

Brax turned toward the door, then paused, looking at Trevor over his shoulder. "Ollie already knows it as an agent, but remind him as

Courtney's friend that a slow start like this doesn't mean we won't find her. It just means we're eliminating the bad choices early on."

"I will," Trevor said. "But thanks for the reminder."

"Yeah, well, sometimes it's hard to remember that Ollie is a victim here, too." Brax's shoulders rose and fell, his expression haunted "I know a little bit about that."

"I'm sorry," Trevor said, remembering reading in Brax's file that he'd seen his girlfriend murdered. It seemed as if everyone on the team had stared into Hell at one time or another.

He hurried downstairs to dive into work and checked in with Liam first. "We're chugging along. Interviewing everyone significant in her life, and a few select insignificants, too. We've got a team on that. A team looking at her banking and credit card statements. She took a vacation about a month ago—one of those all-inclusive islands. Denny's working with the folks in Mexico. You can see it all in the night report."

"Good work."

"Still nothing on tracking the car," he added. "We're running through permutations for the plate, but that's going to take time even with access to Stark's servers."

"Have we been searching the street traffic?"

"Sure," Liam said. "Time-coordinated footage of Laurel Canyon and Ventura. No sign of a car with a plate sporting those initial letters."

*Dammit.* It made no sense. "Okay. Keep at it. Maybe a shadow. Or blocked by another car. Maybe it turned —"

He cut himself off, tilting his head to one side as he tried to will the idea to manifest. It was right there—and it was brilliant, if he did say so himself.

"The parking lot," he said. "What if it was always in the parking lot?"

"I'm not following."

"We've been assuming the captor's car turned in off of Laurel. But what if it actually came from the opposite end of the parking lot, way down at the end?"

In a land of parallel street parking, this free parking lot located behind the grocery store and the various shared-wall retailers that lined Ventura Boulevard was an oasis. One section was dedicated to the Von's, but the rest was for the retailers.

And there were a shit ton of parking spaces back there.

Trevor could picture what had happened, and he laid it out for Liam. The perp had parked in the lot and waited. Then he'd driven through the lot toward Laurel Canyon, made a U-turn in the lot rather than turning onto the street, then eased in the opposite direction, heading back in the direction he'd come from—and also toward Courtney.

From the camera's perspective, though, it appeared that he'd entered the lot from the Laurel Canyon entrance only moments before Courtney was abducted.

"Smart son-of-a-bitch," Trevor said.

"We haven't proved it yet," Liam pointed out.

"We will." He gave his friend's back a friendly pat. "Pull video from the far end of the parking lot. Find me when you have it."

"You got it," Liam said, as Trevor moved on to check in with the rest of his people, all of whom were working their tails off to find Courtney. It was a good team, made up of some of the top-notch operatives in the country. They were smart, well-trained, and tireless.

And they still had next to nothing.

With a sigh, Trevor rubbed his temples. *Soon,* he thought. *Something would break soon.*

In the meantime, he'd go find Ollie and give him an update, especially on the license plate and his parking lot theory. With any luck, they'd have registration information within the hour.

Since Ollie wasn't downstairs with the team, he assumed he was on the third floor snagging a latte, but he wasn't there, either.

Trevor was about to shoot him a text when Damien stepped out of the owner's suite in a suit that probably cost more than Trevor's car, his phone in his hand as he presumably scrolled through the day's schedule.

He glanced up, saw Trevor, and slipped the phone into his jacket pocket. "Where are we today?"

"Slow progress, but we may have some news soon. A new angle on the partial plate."

"Good." He sighed with a small shake of his head. "Ollie must be out of his mind. I've been there. That feeling of helplessness?" His dual-colored eyes seemed to blaze. "I wouldn't wish that on my worst enemy."

Trevor nodded, remembering how gutted Damien had been when Anne had been taken, then again when Nikki disappeared. "I know. And, yeah, it's eating at him." He glanced around the third floor. "I actually came up here to find him, but I haven't seen him anywhere. You?"

"The gym," Damien said. "I think he wanted to burn off some steam."

"Makes sense. First floor, right?"

"Right. Just past the kitchen."

"Thanks," Trevor said, glancing sideways to the only kitchen he was familiar with. But he continued on down to the first floor, albeit a bit confused. Then he remembered that Ollie once told him the house had been built with a huge, commercial quality kitchen that was supposed to be the primary cooking area, with the third floor being used only when entertaining.

Another example of something not turning out the way you expected—but still ending up for the better.

Because, yeah, when he'd first met Ollie, he'd only expected they'd be friends. Why pine for more when the guy wasn't into men? But then things shifted. And in the most satisfying of ways.

Now, Ollie was his.

At least, he hoped he was.

He frowned. That damned niggle of doubt kept popping up no matter how much he told himself that he was channeling Greg. And Greg, frankly, didn't even deserve to be in Trevor's head.

He found Ollie in a gym that was bigger and better equipped than the gym Trevor belonged to near his condo. He supposed he shouldn't be surprised. After all, Damien could afford to fill the massive room with the best, and considering his first career as a professional athlete, it made sense he'd want to stay in shape.

Ollie was on the far side of the room, sitting on a bench in front of a glass wall that looked out over the Malibu hills and the distant beach. His back was to the room, so Trevor couldn't see what he was doing, but he seemed to be looking at something. Probably his phone.

Trevor took a step toward him, then another and another, with each step expecting Ollie to notice him. To turn around. To smile.

But Ollie just sat, and after one more step, Trevor saw why. *Courtney.*

Ollie's tablet was in his lap, and even from where he stood, Trevor could see her image. A candid shot in a park. She was bending over to pluck a daisy, and someone—presumably Ollie—had caught the image of her as she turned to face the camera.

It was a sweet image full of innocence and laughter. There was love there, too. He could see it in her eyes. In the framing of the photo. In the photo's very existence.

And he could see it in the way Ollie's fingers softly stroked the image. Even without seeing Ollie's face, there was no discounting the depth of his emotion. And while Trevor would move heaven and earth to get Courtney back, right then the jealousy that ripped through him was almost debilitating.

*Get a grip, Barone.*

He must have made a sound, because Ollie stiffened, locked the tablet screen, then turned. For a moment, his expression was entirely blank, and that emptiness felt like blackness inside Trevor. Then he smiled, wide and genuine even if it was a little sad. Ollie held out his hand, and Trevor moved to take it, more relieved than he ought to be. But that was just a testament to how hard he'd fallen.

"I woke up alone," he said, proud of how the words sounded detached and reasonable.

"Sorry about that." Ollie's expression seemed almost embarrassed. "You looked so peaceful, I didn't want wake you."

Trevor took another step closer. "You okay?" He nodded at the tablet. "Squeezing in some work?"

"Just, you know, reading." He tugged his hand free. "Clearing my mind."

"Right." Trevor had to force the word out. "That makes sense." *Fuck it.* "I was just tracking you down to give you an update."

"You've learned something?"

"Getting closer." He explained his assumption that the car had been in the parking lot the entire time. "If I'm right, we may have the full plate number soon."

Ollie's relief was palpable as tension seemed to retreat from his whole body. "That's something. Tug on that string, and surely it will loosen more threads."

Trevor shoved his hands in his pockets. "That's the plan." He started to take a step toward Ollie, then stopped. Dammit, he didn't need this. He was heading up this investigation, he needed his head on straight, not all twisted up because of relationship drama.

*Relationship? They'd only fucked. At least that's how it looked like Ollie saw it.*

He sighed. When had he become such a besotted teen?

The answer was easy enough: when he fell for Ollie. As for when he became an insecure mass of hormones, well, that was when he saw the expression on Ollie's face after he'd shut down the tablet and turned around.

Guilt. And regret. And infinite sadness.

*He still loved her.*

Ollie—a straight man until five minutes ago—still loved the girl he'd dated for about a decade.

And how on earth did Trevor compete with that?

## Chapter Twelve

Ollie frowned, trying to read Trevor's expression, a cold knot of worry building in his gut. "What aren't you telling me? Has the kidnapper made contact again? Do you have reason to think he's harmed her?"

Trevor's eyes widened. "No. Why do you think—"

"Do *not* try to shield me from this case," Ollie said, striding toward him, furious at the thought that anything—*anything*—about Courtney's kidnapping was being withheld from him. "Just because we're sleeping together doesn't mean you get to decide what I can and cannot handle."

"Are we?" Trevor's chin lifted as he took a step forward.

"Are we?" Ollie repeated, completely confused. "Are we what?"

"Sleeping together." The words were hard, as if Trevor had to grind them out between his teeth.

"Um, yeah, aren't we?" Ollie was having a hard time understanding why he was picking up a weird vibe from Trevor. "I mean, we didn't get a lot of actual sleep last night, but still. We are. Aren't we?" He flashed a quick grin, feeling the need to lighten the tension, but not understanding why.

"Yeah," Trevor said. "Of course we are."

The words sounded sincere, but Trevor hadn't come closer. He hadn't reached out to touch Ollie, as he frequently had even before they'd slept together. And he still wasn't meeting Ollie's eyes.

What was going on?

"So, were you just coming down here to find me?" He glanced at his watch, then winced when he saw the time. "Right. Sorry. I lost track of time. Almost time for the briefing." In fact, there was a full thirty minutes before the briefing, and while Damien's house might be huge, it didn't take that long to go from the gym to where the command center was set up on the first floor.

"Right. I should go get my ducks in order before I stand up there in front of the entire team."

Ollie nodded, waiting for Trevor to suggest they walk back together.

"So, I'll see you there, okay?"

The words were like a punch in the gut, and Ollie desperately hoped that Trevor hadn't seen him wince. "Yeah. Of course. I'll be there in a sec."

"Great. Good." And on that auspicious note, Trevor left.

*What the actual fuck?*

Slowly, Ollie sank back down to the bench, because his knees weren't quite up to the task of keeping him upright.

He was still sitting there, baffled, when Leah hurried in, stopping short when she saw him. "Oh! Sorry. I didn't realize anyone was down here. I wanted to get in a quick ten minutes on the treadmill before the meeting."

Ollie stood, his knees proving to be up to the task. "I'll get out of your hair and let you have some privacy."

"I can run in public." She grabbed a towel from the stack by the water cooler and slung it around her neck as she headed for the treadmill. She got on, then started the conveyor. He watched as she took off at a slow jog, then looked over her shoulder to meet his eyes. She frowned, then pushed the button to stop the machine.

"Okay, what the fuck is going on?"

Ollie's eyes widened. "Excuse me?"

"You look like someone just ripped your guts out, and I bumped into Trevor on my way here, and he looks like he just ran over his favorite dog. So, I ask again. What's going on here?"

"What did Trevor say when you asked him that?"

She grinned. "Fair enough. He said you were down here worrying about Courtney."

"That about sums it up. She must be terrified. I can't even imagine. Part of me hopes they have her drugged and asleep, but that's dangerous too. I just wish there was some way to know that she was actually unharmed and alive."

"Yeah. I get that. You loved her, and you're worried about her."

"I did, and I am." Ollie frowned. "Wait a sec. He actually told you I was worrying about Courtney?"

"Yeah."

"I didn't tell him that. I mean, I suppose it's obvious, after all that's why we're all here. But..." He trailed off with a shrug, remembering.

"What?"

Ollie frowned. "It's just that before he got here, I was looking at an old picture of her. One I took a few weeks before she broke it off completely. And rightfully so," he added. "The idea of the two of us together was good in theory, but not in practice. I love her, but I don't think I was ever in love with her, you know?"

"I do know," Leah said. "I'm not sure Trevor does."

"What are you talking about?"

"If he told me that you were worrying about Courtney, then he must have seen you looking at that picture, right?"

Ollie nodded slowly, his stomach feeling a little queasy. "Yeah. He was behind me. He could have easily seen over my shoulder before I shut down the tablet." He grimaced, mentally slapping his head. "Why didn't he say something?"

"Oh come on, Ollie. You know why."

"Yeah. I guess I do." He sighed. "I need to go talk to him."

He started toward the door.

"Wait."

He turned back to face Leah. "What?"

"You know he's in love with you, right?"

The words shot through Ollie like warm sugar, and he nodded. That blunt statement not terrifying him at all. "He hasn't said so. But, yeah. I know."

"I think you love him too, but I don't know you well enough yet to be certain. If you do, you need to let him know. And if you don't, you need to let him know."

She tilted her head, looking him up and down as if sizing him up. "For what it's worth, I think you two are good together. But I swear to God if you hurt him, I will rip your throat out myself."

Ollie grinned. "Noted."

He started to walk away again, then stopped and looked back at her, his smile even broader. "I believe you, by the way. And I think I respect you now just a little bit more."

\* \* \* \*

It was a testament to their professionalism that they both got through the meeting. Trevor directed the briefing with a firm hand, cutting through the long reports to get to the core information, re-assigning tasks, and leading the brainstorming for where to go next with the ease of an expert.

Despite the fact that Trevor never held eye contact, watching him was one hell of a turn-on. There was little Ollie appreciated more than competence, and Trevor had it in spades. Not only that, but by the time the briefing ended, even though they'd made slow progress—and still had no firm leads on the perp or Courtney's location—Ollie actually felt hopeful. This was an organization and a leader with the skill and the people to find her and rescue her. She was in good hands.

And, knowing that, he justified his plan to pull Trevor away from work long enough to clear the air.

"How are you holding up?" Brax asked after the briefing, intercepting Ollie on his way to Trevor's side.

"Not the best week of my life, but we'll get her back."

"We will," Brax said firmly. "And we'll get her back alive."

He started to turn, clearly intending to return to work, but Ollie reached out, touching his elbow to stop him. "You okay?" He didn't know the full story, but he'd heard whispers back in the day about a tragedy with Brax's girlfriend. "I've heard … okay, nothing specific, but…"

For a moment, Brax was silent, and Ollie feared he'd overstepped his boundaries. "I saw them grab her," he said. "My girlfriend, Sabrina. We were both twenty, and I couldn't do a thing. Not when they grabbed her. Not when they killed her."

Ollie reached out, his hand closing over Brax's forearm. "I'm so sorry."

Brax drew in a breath, his head tilted to the floor. Then he straightened, his clear blue eyes meeting Ollie's. "One day, I'll find them. One day, I'll kill them."

"Yeah," Ollie said, thinking of what he'd do if anyone hurt Courtney. Even more, if anyone hurt Trevor. "You will."

For a moment, they both just stood there, then a small smile touched Brax's lips. "Thanks, buddy. We're going to find her. You know that, right?"

"We will," Ollie said firmly. "No other outcome will do."

"You've got that right," Brax said, then gave him a little salute before heading over to check in with Denny.

Ollie caught Trevor's eye, then cocked his head, indicating that Trevor should follow. For a moment, he actually thought Trevor would refuse. But then he fell in behind Ollie.

Relieved, Ollie led the way down the hall, then hooked a right into another hall that led to the girls' playroom. It was empty now—Ollie assumed Bree was with the girls in the third-floor kitchen—and he indicated for Trevor to have a seat...on one of the tiny plastic chairs.

He frowned. "I swear, the last time I was in here, there were some adult chairs, too."

"Sure there were," Trevor said with a chuckle. "You planned this just so I wouldn't be at my best."

"So neither of us would," Ollie said, straddling his own kid-sized chair. "But right now, I don't think either of us is, anyway."

"Want to cut to the chase and explain that? In case you hadn't noticed, I have an investigation to run."

"I noticed that. Not entirely sure why you're in charge, though. Under the circumstances."

Trevor leaned back, his brows rising. "Circumstances?"

"You being so fucking clueless, I mean."

For a moment, Trevor's face was a study in shock. Then his hands clutched the back of the minuscule chair. "All right. I'm listening."

Ollie drew in a breath, then leaned forward, his arms resting on the back of the chair as his hands reached for Trevor's. "I'm not in love with her. I'm not entirely sure I ever was. But I do care for her. I do worry about her. If I hadn't screwed her over by not letting her go long before she dumped me, I think we would have been close friends. Now, I just want to find her. To make sure she's safe."

He paused, waiting for Trevor to say something. When he didn't, he continued. "I was only looking at her picture, Trev. I was worried. I *am* worried. But I don't love her like that." He drew in a breath for courage. "But I do love you."

He saw the flicker in Trevor's eyes. "Love?"

"Yeah." It was remarkably—terrifyingly—easy to get the word out. "Love." He lifted a shoulder. "I think I've been in love with you for a while, actually. Honestly, it's a little disconcerting."

Trevor's brows rose. "Disconcerting?"

"Me. Falling for a guy. Never expected it. And now here I am, putting my fragile ego on the line, and I don't even know if the guy feels the same."

Trevor nodded slowly. "Yeah. I can see how that could be awkward." He eased closer, and when he spoke again, his voice was low. "I'm probably not supposed to be telling you this, but I have it on pretty good authority that he loves you, too."

Ollie fought the smile that tugged at his lips. "Is that a fact?"

"Who can tell amidst all the rumors," Trevor said airily, "but that's the word on the street."

They shared a smile as a thousand tons of weight that had settled on Ollie's shoulders finally evaporated. And when Trevor tilted the tiny chair forward so he could capture Ollie's mouth, it felt as if they were finally a team again.

As soon as they rescued Courtney, they could slide into the process of figuring out how to merge their lives together.

Honestly, Ollie couldn't think of anything he'd ever looked forward to as much.

"I guess I proved my own theorem," Trevor said.

"What do you mean?"

"Relationships. Making you crazy. Ours spun me out a bit."

Ollie chuckled. "It did, didn't it? But I'd say you landed okay. Only a few bumps and bruises, and—*Oh*."

He practically leaped to his feet, knocking over the child's chair in the process. Trevor was on his feet in an instant, too. "What? Ollie? What is it?"

"We've been right all along, but we didn't realize *how* we were right."

Trevor shook his head, his hand twirling as if urging Ollie to spit the story out faster. "It is about me. Or, I think it is. What if it's just not about my cases? What if it's about me and Courtney?"

Trevor shook his head slowly. "Not following you."

"Relationships making you crazy. What if we should be looking for someone who was in a relationship with her?"

"What does that have to do with you?" His brows rose. "Unless you're our perp."

"Funny man. No, I'm thinking someone she dated when we were on-again/off-again."

Trevor nodded slowly. "We've been looking at men in her life since you two broke up. But we haven't gone earlier." He stood. "You may be right. Let's go see if Denny and Mario can push this to the top of their lists."

"It feels right," Ollie said as they hurried toward the command center. But even as he enjoyed the high of possibly having latched onto a lead, he couldn't help the dark stab of guilt. Because if he was right, then he was the catalyst, and Courtney's life was in danger because once upon a time, he'd been too much of an asshole to walk away and stay away.

# Chapter Thirteen

Twenty-eight hours later, the entire team was exhausted. They took longer shifts, re-interviewed people who knew Courtney, and drilled deeper into her computer to recover and do a second pass through old emails, texts, contacts, and anything else that might be useful.

They scoured her calendars again and dug through her apartment looking for anything they might have missed the first go-round. Old journals, old ledger pages, even old Girl Scout calendars tossed in the back of a closet. Anything that might have a hint as to who they were chasing. They found little; why would they? The team had picked over her place with a magnifying glass the first time they'd gone through.

They worked hard and fast, but as the hours rolled by, the knot in Ollie's gut tightened. They still weren't making enough progress, and the time for the ransom drop was coming up. Once they made that drop, they lost control of the situation.

The kidnapper might release her. Or he might just take the money and run, leaving Courtney trapped in whatever hellhole he was keeping her locked up in. They'd follow the money, of course—they'd do everything imaginable to capture the son-of-a-bitch—but plans could go wrong. Bad guys sometimes won.

And far too often, kidnap victims were never recovered.

*Not today.* Ollie took a deep breath, forcing himself to stay calm and focused. Wherever Courtney was, she was still alive, and Ollie was determined that she'd stay that way.

"Hey," Trevor said, coming up behind Ollie. He slipped his arms around Ollie's waist, and Ollie leaned back, grateful for both the touch and the emotional support. "You hanging in there?"

"I'm trying to. But the clock keeps ticking down."

"I know," Trev said. "We all do. But we're working both ends.

Tracking down the bastard who took her, and specing out the mission surrounding the actual drop. If it comes down to it, we'll apprehend him then. Either way, we'll find her. We'll get her back, Ollie. And we'll get her back safe."

Ollie damn sure hoped so, but with each second that passed, the dark cloud of fear that had surrounded him since he learned about the kidnapping pressed in tighter and tighter until it was close to smothering him.

He caught Denny's eye across the room, where she was jamming at the keyboard, once again parsing through the security footage second by second for any hint as to who might have taken Courtney.

Slowly, she shook her head. *Nothing.*

Ollie closed his eyes, allowing himself one more moment of fear before forcing his mind to focus again. Fear wouldn't help her. Nothing but intellect and action could help her now, and he wasn't going to fail on either count.

"Go over everything again," he said. "We're missing something. This guy is part of her life, or he was. There must be some sort of record of him." He looked around the room to see if anybody was going to argue. Thankfully, nobody did. "And each of you need to grab an hour of downtime." He needed them fresh. Their minds clicking, putting the pieces of the puzzle together.

"Ollie's right," Trevor said, then pointed to Mario, Quince, and Liam. "You three go grab an hour."

"You, too," Ollie said. "You skipped your last break."

Trevor hesitated.

"Go," Ollie insisted. "You're on the strike team, you need to be fresh."

"So do you."

Ollie shook his head, "My only job is carrying the money."

"Being a walking, talking target is what you mean."

"It is what it is."

"Ollie..."

"Go. I'm going to work with Denny."

Trevor frowned, but nodded. "One hour. Then I'm back, and it's your turn."

"Yes, sir," Ollie said with a salute that had Trevor rolling his eyes.

He wished he could go crash with Trevor now, but that was just selfishness. He'd be more help to Denny, and they both needed actual sleep.

The thought made him smile. They were together now—truly together, with the whole world knowing. Or as much of the world that was currently bunking at Chez Stark. Which, as far as Ollie was concerned, was pretty much everyone.

Except for his mom and dad and Courtney, the people under this roof made up his entire world. They were there for him, which meant they were there for Courtney.

They were a team. All of them.

And that felt pretty damn nice.

\* \* \* \*

"So what do you think?" Ollie asked, his arm outstretched to show off his house, now fully refurbished.

"It's incredible. You did an amazing job."

"We did," Ollie said, moving closer to take Trevor's hands. "I'm glad you're moving in."

Trevor's pulse picked up its tempo. "Yeah. Me, too."

"Come on," Ollie said, releasing Trevor's hands and cocking his head. "Let me show you where you're sleeping."

"Sleeping...?"

"Or not sleeping." Ollie's eyes glinted with amusement. "I have plans for you."

"Oh, yeah?" Trevor could feel his whole body heating up, anticipation rising.

"Most definitely." Ollie climbed onto the bed, then straddled Trevor before moving higher and higher until his lips brushed Trevor's own. "So many plans."

"Tell me," Trevor demanded, barely able to breathe, his fingers digging into the sheets, desperate for this man's words, his touch, his cock.

"I'm going to kiss you," Ollie said. "I'm going to whisper into your ear how much I want you. How much I crave the feel of your skin against mine. How deep I want to kiss you. How desperate I am for the taste of your cock. And most of all, how much I want you to fuck me. To own me."

"Yes." It was the only word he could manage through the haze of lust that was surrounding him. "Ollie, oh, god, yes."

"I want to feel you explode inside of me. I want you to whisper that you love me. That you need me. That I'm everything to you. And I'll whisper it all back to you, too. Every word. Every emotion. Every decadent touch that you think means everything. You'll have them all. For then."

"For then?" He tried to sit up, but Ollie's weight on his chest kept him flat on his back. Panic bubbled up, but he told himself to breath. "What do you mean, 'for then.'"

"Just like it sounds," Ollie said, easing back so that he was sitting upright, straddling Trevor's waist. "You'll have it for then. Maybe a little longer." He reached out and tapped Trevor's nose. "But you can't be greedy, babe. You can't expect me to stay. There are other fish in the sea. Other men in the world."

He leaned forward, his hands stroking Trevor's bare chest, then down to circle his cock. "Other men with hard abs and hard cocks. Women, too. Soft in all the right places. Do you think I want to miss out? Do you think I'm ready to settle? Now, when I've barely opened the door? There's a whole world out there—literally. You can't ask me to just close that door. Not after you opened it for me."

No. No, no, no.

Trevor tried to scream the word, but he couldn't. Ollie's lips were on his, the kiss drawing out his soul, stealing his reason, making him weak. Alone. Lost.

His eyes fluttered shut, and a cold chill settled over him. It took a moment to realize that Ollie was no longer on top of him, and the cold had settled in his absence.

Ollie!

Trevor tried to scream, but the sound was only in his head. He couldn't get it out into the world. Couldn't call to Ollie. Couldn't argue for him to stay. Couldn't tell him that he loved him. Needed him.

He could only look around in horror at the empty room. At the harsh lights that made the bedroom feel like a jail cell.

He could only feel the well of loneliness looming deep within him as he cried out, Ollie, Ollie, Ollie.

"Hey, hey, I'm right here. Come on. It's time to leave."

"Don't leave." He heard the words, but he couldn't wrap his head around who was talking.

"Trevor—Trevor, wake up." Hands on his arms. The brush of fingertips over his cheek. The voice so, so gentle. "Come on, wake up. We found him. We're leaving in two minutes."

"Don't—don't leave."

"Dammit, Trev. Wake up. We found him. We need to go."

*Found him.*

Found who?

Ollie?

But it was Ollie talking to him. Ollie saying goodbye. That he was leaving. That he was walking away just like Greg had done.

So who had they found?

The words made no sense—until they did.

He sat up with a jolt, reality hitting him like that damn Acme anvil hitting the coyote. "You found him."

"And we're going now. Come or stay, but we're out of time."

"I'm in." He'd slept in his slacks, so he slid out of bed, shoved his feet into his shoes, and grabbed his shirt as they hurried from the room.

"You okay?" Ollie asked, glancing sideways at him as they hurried toward the front door where two Range Rovers were waiting.

Trevor nodded, tucking his shirt in as they sprinted to their vehicle. "Catch me up," he demanded once they were settled in the back. He reached for Ollie's hand. "How'd we find the guy?"

Ollie ignored Trevor's hand, instead leaning forward to say something to Brax, who was driving. When he settled back, he kept his body angled toward Trev's, his hands on the slim binder with the mission specs.

"It was Quince who tracked him," Ollie said.

"But you remembered," Mario pointed out. "I'd found a ticket stub for *Wicked*—you know, the musical—being used as a bookmark. Didn't think much of it, but logged it. And that was enough for Ollie."

"What did you remember?" Trevor asked.

"A guy," Ollie said simply. "She never talked much about who she went out with when we were in an off-again phase, but one time we were talking about *Wicked*—I think it was touring—and she mentioned that a bi-coastal guy she'd gone out with had promised to get them front row seats. But she was back with me, so that wouldn't happen." He shrugged. "And then about eight months later we were on-again, and I saw the souvenir sweatshirt at her place."

"She'd gone to New York to see him."

"Yeah. I found out they'd seen each other several times when we were apart. I mentioned him not long ago, actually. She was going to Manhattan for some article she was writing, so I asked if she was seeing that guy."

"Was she?"

"Nope. Told me she'd shut it down. He wanted to get serious, but she didn't."

Trevor nodded slowly. "So maybe he's the jealous type."

"That's what I thought. But she never told me his full name. Just Bobby. But Quince is a god among men and managed to track him down."

"Robert Ellis Fulton," Mario said, speaking for Quince who was in the second vehicle. "Damn solid work, too. Once we had that, I was able to dig in. We're heading to his LA house—he's in Valley Village."

"With luck," Leah said, sliding into the conversation, "he's holding Courtney there and this will be over before it's begun. A little less luck, and we've got him, then Quince can work his magic to tell us where Courtney is being held."

Trevor nodded. Ollie had probably never seen Quince in action, but he'd had that privilege. He didn't know if it was MI6 training or something else, but Quince was better with a hypodermic and the power of suggestion than anyone else he'd run across in his years doing this kind of work. "Quince is amazing," he told Ollie, reaching over to take his hand. "If we have to get into Bobby's head, he can totally manage that."

He squeezed Ollie's fingers, more relieved than he should be when Ollie squeezed back, though the gesture seemed a little half-hearted.

*Get a grip,* he ordered himself. One bad dream didn't mean the world was crumbling beneath him.

"There's another reason we're one-hundred percent convinced this is our guy," Ollie said, pulling his hand free of Trevor's as he clenched his hands together in what Trevor recognized as a nervous habit.

Trevor frowned, focusing on those hands as trepidation built. "Tell me."

"Angelina Castor."

Trevor shook his head. "Should I know that name?"

"No," Ollie said, then drew a breath. "She's dead."

Trevor heard the crack in Ollie's voice, and knew he was terrified for Courtney. "She used to date Bobby, and she died two days after she broke up with him. Accidental fall from her balcony. Except the balcony railing came up to her ribcage."

Trevor reached over, then took Ollie's hand again. "She's not Courtney."

The pain in Ollie's face when he met Trevor's eyes was like a gut-punch to the soul. "Isn't she?"

"We'll catch him. We'll get her back. Don't go worst case until we have to. Stay positive."

Ollie nodded, then tugged his hand free before rubbing his face with his palms even as Trevor's throat went tight.

He felt it, then. That almost-forgotten sensation that preceded a panic attack. The way his breath caught in his throat, as if something was blocking his airway. The increased tempo of his pulse. The fine beads of sweat gathering at the back of his neck and on his upper lip.

*Stop it.*

He ordered himself to relax. To count to ten, then breathe in through his nose.

Once, twice, third times a charm.

Ollie turned to him, his brow furrowed. "You okay?"

Trevor waved the words away, then pressed his fingers to his temple. "A little carsick. Nothing to worry about."

"We're here," Brax said, sliding into a spot in a tree-lined neighborhood. "The house with the blue trim."

Ollie pulled out his radio, contacting the first car. "Move in," he ordered. "Team two covering the exits."

Trevor eyed him. "We're not the first team?"

Ollie shook his head. Just one firm shake, and Trevor realized that Ollie feared what the team would find in there. Knowing that, it was all Trevor could do not to pull him close for a hug. Not now, though. Not when Ollie was focused on the mission.

*Not when Ollie seemed to be pulling away minute by minute, second by second.*

He forced the thought down, along with the knot that was once again blocking his throat. Dammit, he didn't need this shit. He was past this shit. He'd taken administrative leave after Greg walked. He'd gotten himself under control. And there was no fucking way he was losing that control again.

"Come on," he said to Mario and Leah. "We'll take the rear of the house. "Ollie, you and Brax cover the front."

"Roger," Brax said, as he and Ollie opened their doors. Trevor didn't look back. Didn't want to think about Ollie not brushing his fingers in a silent goodbye. Not watching when Trevor disappeared around to the back.

Not caring about anything but the mission.

Yeah, he was an asshole, all right. Because right then, the mission was all any of them should be caring about.

"You okay?" Mario's whispered question caught him by surprise.

"A little off my game," Trevor admitted. "Not enough sleep. I'll be fine." He glanced back, saw Mario's eyes narrow before the tech genius crouched in front of the back door as he lifted the snap gun to unlock the deadbolt.

"If the man says he's fine, he's fine," Leah said firmly, then added, "We're going in," as Mario shot them a thumbs up and put his hand on the knob.

"Roger that." Ollie's voice. And then Trev and Leah were on either side of Mario. Mario counted it off, and on three they entered, Trevor high and Leah low, their weapons at the ready.

"Clear," Leah said, leading the way through the kitchen to where it opened into a living area. They maneuvered in further, clearing the rooms as they went, Trevor praying they'd find the son-of-a-bitch. Even better, that they'd find Courtney.

They didn't. Not the woman, anyway. But they found her purse, and the moment they did, Trevor watched as Ollie's stoic expression crumbled, and the man he loved fell to his knees, the tears flowing like water.

# Chapter Fourteen

"It's going to be okay. We'll find her. We'll do the drop. We'll follow his rules, and we will find her."

Trevor's soft words surrounded Ollie, but he found no comfort in them. All he could think was that this was his fault. He'd kept drawing her back to him, and then ripping it all down again. And each time this guy must have been getting more and more frustrated. *Bitch, you think you can just use me in between? You think I'll put up with that?*

He could practically hear Bobby's voice in his head. The angry words. The violent temper, hidden under a surface that seemed so even and personable.

He knew the type. For that matter, he'd taken classes on the type when he was in training.

The type was dangerous.

And now Bobby had Courtney.

"Dammit, Ollie, look at me," Trevor demanded. "We will get her back."

"All of this," Ollie said, feeling like he was being sucked into a deep, dark pit. "I can lay it all at my feet. If I hadn't kept pulling her back—"

"You know better, Agent McKee," Trevor snapped. "Don't you even think about going there. This is about his particular psychosis, not about your relationship with Courtney, and you damn well know it. So quit feeling sorry for yourself, Agent. There's a woman out there who needs your help. You don't have the luxury of melting down."

Ollie nodded, Trevor's words finally pounding through the fear and self-loathing that had washed over him like a tsunami.

"I know. I know. I just—I just need a moment." He had to pull himself together. Had to shut down the emotions, rely on his training, and do the job.

Trevor reached out to take his hand, but the moment their fingers brushed, Ollie drew back sharply. He couldn't—not right then. Trevor was his refuge; the place where he could break down and pour out all his fears. All his guilt.

But he didn't have the luxury of doing that right now, and a single touch could start the boulder downhill, and then he'd never stop. He'd be lost in grief, and that would be no help to Courtney.

No, he had to be professional. He had to concentrate on his training.

He had to do the job.

Slowly, he drew in a breath, then nodded, as much to himself as to Trevor. "Okay," he said. "I'm ready. Go gather the team."

For a moment, Trevor only looked at him, his expression dark and a little sad. And why wouldn't it be? They didn't have the victim safely tucked away and the kidnapper was still on the loose. They were going to have to deliver the ransom, and that was the riskiest maneuver in a kidnapping. Trevor knew that as well as Ollie did.

Not a good situation. But Ollie wasn't thinking about that. On the contrary, he was determined that he would see Courtney again. And when he did, she'd be alive and unharmed.

"Right," Trevor said, not quite meeting Ollie's eyes. "Five minutes. We'll convene on the driveway." He glanced around Bobby's small bungalow. "Better outside. There's a chance this place is wired."

"Good thinking," Ollie said as they moved outside and into the front yard. "In fact, let's get a team in here to sweep for that. If Bobby is listening in, maybe we can trace it back."

"On it," Trevor said, then moved away. This time, he didn't reach for Ollie, and even though Ollie couldn't afford the distraction of Trevor's touch—even though he needed to cling to pure professionalism if he was going to get through this—that simple absence weighed on him.

Outside, the two teams gathered in the driveway, speaking in low voices to avoid being overheard by any of the neighbors.

"We have two hours until the ransom drop," Trevor said. "Unless anyone else has a better idea, we're going to move forward as planned. Ollie will take the money in, leave it at the drop site. We'll have eyes on for as long as it takes, but hopefully he'll make a move to get the cash within twenty-four hours. According to his instructions, once he's acquired the cash, he'll let us know where to find Courtney."

He glanced around at the group, his eyes skimming over Ollie without even hesitating. "We'll follow the money, but the hostage is our priority. Questions?"

There were none, and so the group split up, heading back into the Range Rovers to both plan and head to the drop site.

The site itself was a men's room inside the Sherman Oaks Galleria. They parked a half mile away where a variety of base model cars were parked and ready for them, courtesy of ASAC Horowitz. The team switched from the Range Rovers to the cars, then each driver engaged in some evasive maneuvers before parking at the shopping center.

"You ready?" Trevor asked, his hands tight on the steering wheel, as if he was gluing himself in place.

"Yeah." Ollie drew a breath. "Yeah, I've got this." He reached over, then pressed his hand to Trevor's thigh. He wanted to pull him in for a kiss. For support.

But he couldn't. Not if he wanted to keep himself centered. Right then, he needed absolute focus.

One more breath, then he nodded. "Okay. Keep a close eye. I'm not keen on being taken out by one to the head." Presumably the kevlar he wore under his shirt would take care of one to the chest, but he wasn't wearing a kevlar skull cap. Wouldn't matter anyway. Any self-respecting sniper would get him right between the eyes.

*Rambling.*

He forced his nerves back down, then opened the door. Trevor reached for him, then squeezed his hand before he could pull away, and he squeezed back, afraid the touch would knock him off his game, but still needing it as much as Trevor did.

"In. Out. Done. You've got this," Trevor said. "You'll make the drop, we'll get the address, and Courtney will be fine."

"And Bobby?"

"We've got eyes everywhere," Trevor reminded him. "We'll track him down. But priority one is Courtney, and we're making that happen today. Right?"

"Hell, yes," Ollie said, then slipped out of the car. He opened the back door, grabbed the bags that Damien had prepped, and headed into the mall.

He couldn't see any of the team—they were all too damn good—but he knew they were watching. He walked in through one of the main entrances, only to find the place relatively empty. Once a popular destination, it almost seemed abandoned.

Worked out great for the good guys, Ollie thought. Easier to keep eyes on the target.

He found the restroom easily enough then, entered, his stomach in knots since that was the one area in the mall without eyes.

It was completely empty, and he let out a slow sigh of relief.

His instructions were to put the duffels in the handicapped stall, stacked on the toilet. Then lock the door and crawl out of the stall from underneath.

Someone would be along within the hour to collect the ransom, and they'd leave an envelope with the address where Courtney was being held. Any attempt to follow the bag man would be noted, and a call would be made to the appropriate party, who would quickly and efficiently put a bullet in Courtney's brain.

So, yeah. Ollie was following the rules.

He entered the stall, found that the duffels stacked just fine, and then he locked the door as ordered. He wasn't particularly keen on crawling on the floor, but he had little choice. So he got down, crawled under, then stood upright again to wash his hands.

And then, with only one last look back at the stall with the ransom, he pulled open the door, headed back the way he came, and exited the mall.

He didn't stop until he reached the car he'd arrived in. Trevor was gone—well-hidden inside the mall—and it was Ollie's job to drive away. He did, maneuvering his way to Riverside Drive, then heading east until he was in Valley Village. He puttered around for a while, then turned south onto Laurel Canyon and—in what could only be described as dramatic irony—turned into the Von's parking lot. The very lot where Courtney had been abducted in the first place.

He left his car, switched to another that had already been planted there, changed into board shorts and a faded blue tee, then put on the surfer-blonde wig and ball cap.

After that, he used the key that had been left under the mat to fire up the car and head back to the mall so he could reconnect with the team currently milling about the second floor as they traded off the duty to keep an eye on the men's room.

"Anything?" he said, after putting on the headphone that had also been left for him.

"No takers so far," Leah said. "Not a soul has gone into that restroom."

"I'm on my way."

"See you soon," Trevor said, and just his voice alone made Ollie smile. As soon as this day was over, he was pulling Trevor close and, hopefully, fucking his brains out. He'd need to start with an apology, but surely Trevor would get it. The man knew how distracting he was to Ollie. And today of all days, Ollie had needed to be in full-focus mode.

"We've got something." Brax's voice rang out clear in Ollie's headset. "A kid. Maybe seventeen. Jeans and a red tee. He's heading for the men's room."

"Probably just taking a leak," Leah said.

"Guess we'll see. Yeah, okay, he's in."

Ollie picked up his pace, wanting to get to his station before the kid came out. He didn't make it, and he turned to face the mall's map, then hoped he looked like he was trying to locate a store.

"Bingo." That was Trevor's voice. "He's got the bags and he's on the move."

"On him," Liam said, and Ollie could imagine him and Quince falling in behind the kid, pursuing him to wherever he might be taking the ransom. Which, hopefully, ended up at Bobby's hidey-hole.

"I'm going in," Ollie said, once he'd turned around and saw that neither the kid nor Quince or Liam were anywhere in sight.

"You're cleared," Trevor said. "At your discretion."

Ollie opened the door, then moved into the now unlocked stall where he'd left the money. At first he saw nothing, and he spat out a quick curse, then heard Trevor's sharp intake of breath.

"Nothing?"

"Not a goddamn—wait. Something," he said, seeing the envelope that had been taped beneath the stall's private sink. He tugged it free of the tape, then said a quick prayer before carefully opening the sealed envelope. It contained just a thin strip of paper, and he pulled it out, then closed his eyes and exhaled in relief.

"An address," he said. "We've got an address."

"Report."

He read the address back, and listened as Trevor dismissed Brax and Leah to head that way. "Get back to the car," Trevor said. "We'll be right behind them."

"On my way," Ollie acknowledged, then hurried out of the stall, praying that this wasn't going to all go to shit, and that within the hour, they'd have Courtney safe and sound and back at her home.

* * * *

The address was all the way in Riverside, and since there was no way that Ollie was consigning Courtney to any more time in fear than was necessary, he called the Riverside FBI field office and had a team dispatched.

"Stealth," he stressed. "She's probably alone and bound, locked in. But we don't know that for sure. Call me the moment you have eyes-on."

When he hung up the call, his chest felt tight. "Tell me that wasn't a mistake," he said to Trevor, reaching over to twine their fingers together.

"It wasn't. It's the FBI. They know what they're doing. She's fine, Ollie," he said. "We'll have confirmation soon, but she's fine." He tugged his hand free from Ollie's, then put it on the steering wheel. Ollie was so lost in thought, he barely noticed, his mind too full of worry for Courtney to have room for processing information about the world around him. He was in a car, and they were moving toward her prison. That was all he knew. Right then, that was all he needed to know.

The sharp ring of his phone made him jump, but he hit the button to answer immediately. "You got her?"

"It's Liam. And we lost the money. And Bobby."

Ollie caught Trevor's eye. "What happened?"

"The kid passed if off four times. The last one was Bobby, or if not, it was his doppelgänger. He took the satchels into a men's room in a strip mall in Panorama City. Didn't come out. Turns out the damn thing had a back janitor's entrance. I'm sorry, McKee. That fuck-up's on us."

"You didn't know. You were following protocol. And at least we know he's not with Courtney. I have a local team going after her now. He may have the bills, but he won't have her. And we know who he is. We'll get him."

"We might not," Trevor said after Ollie ended the call. "That kind of cash, he could be halfway to transport out of the country already."

Ollie shook his head. "No. We'll find him. I won't have Courtney living the rest of her life looking over her shoulder."

Trevor stopped at a red light, then turned his attention to Ollie.

"What?"

But Trevor said nothing. Just shook his head. Ollie was about to ask, but the phone rang again. "Tell me," he said when the call connected on the speaker.

"We've got her, sir. Unharmed. He had her tied to a bed. We're cutting her loose right now."

"Check for booby-traps."

"Done and clear. We told her you were on your way. She's unsteady, but clear. And she's looking forward to seeing you."

"Stay with her there. I'll get her statement later, but I need to see her there."

"Affirmative."

"Thank god," Trevor said, but there was something hard under his voice. Frustration about Bobby, Ollie assumed. God knew he was frustrated about the abductor's escape act.

But they'd catch him. Ollie didn't care how long it took, somehow, someway, they'd catch the son-of-a-bitch.

# Chapter Fifteen

"You're really okay?" Ollie stood with his hands on Courtney's shoulders, his gaze skimming over her as if he'd missed some horrible injury.

But she was fine. She was truly fine.

"Yes," she said, her smile in contrast to her puffy and bloodshot eyes. In one burst, she threw herself at him, her arms wrapped tight as he kissed her head. "I knew you'd find me. That's what the FBI does, right?"

"We do indeed," he said, looking over her head to meet Trevor's unreadable eyes.

He frowned, mouthed, *you okay?*

Trevor nodded, then came forward to join them. "We want to keep you under guard for a while," he said, and Ollie wanted to kick himself. Of course, Trevor was focused on practical reality. Ollie was just floating on waves of relief.

"You'll stay with me for a few days. Hopefully we'll have apprehended him but then."

She shuddered, then hugged herself. "I can't believe Bobby did this. I mean, I broke up with him because he was too clingy and, oh, I don't know. He just wasn't right for me. Now I guess he wasn't right in the head. But I never expected anything like this."

"No one does," Ollie assured her, putting his arm around her shoulder and pulling her close. "But it's over now. Or it will be soon. We will get him."

"And if you don't?"

"Then you'll have to live with that. We both will. I don't think he'll try for you again. He doesn't seem like the type. I think he'll take his money and run. But you never know. Can you handle that?"

She swallowed, but nodded. "I guess I won't have much choice. But until we get there, I'm going to root for the good old FBI to catch him."

"And we will do our very best. The SSA, too," he added, shooting another glance at Trevor, and again wondering about the crease in his brow and the frown in his eyes. "We've got good people working this. Right now, I want you to sit down with Denny. Tell her everything you remember. Start from the beginning and just run through it. You never know when something small might help."

She nodded. "Yeah. I can do that."

He shot Denny a quick text and she joined them in the bedroom. "Ready to walk down Memory Lane?"

"Not so much," Courtney said, tucking a lock of dark brown hair behind her ear. "But I guess I have to, anyway."

"It might help," Denny said. "You never know what will." She flashed a smile at Ollie, then cocked her head toward the door. "I'll bring her out to you in a few. You two driving her back to LA?"

"We are," Ollie said. "She's going to bunk at my place for a few days."

"Good," Denny said, with a soft smile toward Courtney. "You'll feel better being with a friend for a while."

"Yeah," Courtney said as she followed Denny out of the room, the door snicking shut as soon as they were across the threshold.

"I can't believe I put her through this," Ollie said, falling into a chair in the dining room.

"It wasn't you. It was him," Trevor said.

"I know. I just—"

"I'm glad she's safe."

Ollie frowned, something in Trevor's tone setting off warning bells. He took a step toward him. "Listen, Trev, you know I'm not in love with her."

"I know. I do."

"She's just staying with me until she's dealt with it. And until we either catch him or cry uncle."

"I know," Trevor said, his tone sharper than Ollie could ever recall. He drew in a shaky breath, then closed his eyes as he simply bent over and breathed.

When he stood up straight again and met Ollie's eyes, the room suddenly went cold.

Ollie shook his head. "Trevor—no."

"I'm sorry, Ollie. You have no idea how sorry I am. But we can't do this. <I>I<\I> can't do this." Tears glistened in his eyes. "I love you. I'm certain of it. But I can't be with you."

And then, without even a backward glance, Trevor walked to the front door, pulled it open, and stepped out of the house, leaving Ollie confused and angry and desperately alone.

* * * *

"You want to talk about it?" Courtney asked, hours later as they settled in Ollie's bedroom in front of the television.

"About what?"

"About whatever you and Trevor talked about while I was with Denny. Because something happened."

"What makes you say that?"

She only cocked her head. "Are you actually asking me that? Me?"

He laughed. Which, frankly, felt pretty good. Even so, he shook his head. "I don't think so. I'd rather just get lost in a movie."

"When have we ever easily agreed on a movie? It will be tomorrow before we decide. Just talk to me. I promise you can do it. We may have sucked at talking about our relationship and feelings and all that, but we could always talk."

"I—" He broke off with a shrug, not sure how to tell his ex-girlfriend that his boyfriend had just dumped him.

"Fine, I'll start. You're dating Trevor, and something happened. I'm guessing the something is me."

Ollie gaped at her. "Dating Trevor. What makes you say that?"

She pinched the bridge of her nose. "I know you, Ol. And I've got eyes." Eyes which she narrowed at him. "Or are you going to tell me I'm wrong?"

He drew in a deep breath. "No," he said. "You're not wrong. Except apparently we aren't dating anymore. And I don't think it had to do with you, specifically, just the girl part of you. His ex-husband left him for a woman. He's gun shy."

Which was pretty damned annoying considering Trevor had been pursuing Ollie with at least as much determination as Ollie had wished he'd had the balls to reciprocate.

"That must've been tough. Probably makes sense that he's gun shy."

"Maybe. I don't know." Ollie frowned. "He told me he gets panic attacks. He lost his mom unexpectedly. I've never seen him have one before—Trev's the most level guy I know. Steady and solid. But I saw one coming on today. And it kills me to know it was because of me."

"But it wasn't. It was because of his mom. And because his ex left him for a woman. None of that's on you."

"I know. But so what?"

"So fight for him."

Ollie managed a sound that resembled a snort.

"Really?" Her brows rose. "That's your response?"

Ollie groaned. "Can we just watch a movie now?"

"No," she said, grabbing the remote and clicking off the television.

"Dammit, Cee. You always do that."

She grinned. "Nice we know each other so well, isn't it? Which means you need to listen to me. About you, I have gee-gobs of wisdom."

"Fine. Fine. Say whatever you want. Just say it and then be quiet so we can either watch a movie or go to sleep."

"Get your ass over to his house and have it out with him."

"I don't think—"

"Shut up. He's nervous, obviously. You need to convince him he doesn't need to be."

"Doesn't he?" Ollie asked. "Look what I did to you."

She took his hand, then gave it a gentle squeeze. "I haven't forgotten. But it's different."

"How?"

Her smile was as sweet as he'd ever seen. "You weren't in love with me."

"I loved you." He heard the defensiveness in his voice and hated himself.

"You did," she agreed. "But you weren't in love with me. You loved me like you love Jamie. Or even Nikki. You would never have ended up with either of them, even if Ryan and Damien had never come on the scene. And it's not because we're women. It's because we're not Trevor."

Ollie could only stare at her. Everything she was saying was absolutely dead on.

Her brow furrowed. "What?"

"He's my lobster."

A wide smile lit her face. "Yeah, I think he is."

Ollie drew in a breath as he took her hand and squeezed. "I do love you."

"I know. Why do you think I kept coming back? And I'm not going anywhere, okay? You'll always be one of my best friends. But I'm fine right now. So go talk to him."

"No way am I leaving you alone."

She lifted a brow. "And you're the only qualified babysitter? What about Leah? Didn't I hear that she's Trevor's roommate? Ask her to come over here, and you'll have him all to yourself."

"I don't remember you being this devious and persistent when we were dating."

She shrugged. "Maybe I only am when I'm pushing for the right match."

He pulled her close and kissed her forehead. "I'm very glad you're still in my life."

"Yeah," she said. "Me too. Especially with a crazy ex wandering around out there."

"Right. Calling Leah now. She's tiny, but she's one hell of a bad ass, and a damn good shot, too."

"And she can entertain me with Trevor stories that you can later bribe me to share."

He laughed, thrilled that after their rollercoaster ride of a relationship, they were finally okay.

He hoped that was a portent. Because one thing he knew for certain, if he lost Trevor now, he'd never recover.

\* \* \* \*

"You forget something?" Trevor asked, answering the call from Leah who'd left about half an hour ago to watch Courtney while Ollie got called into a meeting with Horowitz.

"Nope. All good. I've been talking to Courtney, and I'm just calling to tell you you're a foolish prick."

"Thank you. Appreciate the moral support. Seriously, Leah? What the fuck?"

"I am serious. You're so in love with the guy that you're having panic attacks. You're terrified that he's going to leave you, so you're doing everything in your power to make that actually happen."

"Dammit, Leah. Don't be—"

"Oh, shut up. I know you. I know how you think. And I know that you're being completely stupid about the whole thing."

"Fine. Whatever. Can I just crash now?"

"Not until you tell me that you're going to fight for him. Because, seriously, how often do you feel like that about someone?

*Not that often.*

"You can't just let that go because your delicate little tushie is afraid of getting smacked down. Because, one—grow a pair. And two—that man is head-over-heels for you and he's not going anywhere. And if you can't see it then you need to open your damn eyes."

Somewhere in that ramble, Trevor realized he was smiling.

"You're a good friend, Leah."

"Damn right I am. Which is why I'm telling you that you can't pull away from him. Just the opposite. You need to fight for him."

"You're right."

"I mean, really fight because—wait. I'm right?"

"You are." She was. He loved Ollie. And, yeah, he was terrified that he'd leave, but he'd rather be with Ollie and control the terror than be without him and floundering.

"You're going to fight for him?"

That time he outright laughed. "Yes. You're right. Do I have to tattoo it on my backside?"

"Maybe. Mostly I'm just glad you see it. And that you're ready for a throw down. Because, my charming roomie, Ollie's on his way to you right now. And his agenda is pretty much the same. I recommend make-up sex, you know. Just not on the sofa, okay?"

"Wait, what?"

"You're surprised? The boy's stone deep in love with you. And he and all of his persuasive lawyer skills are on their way over to convince you. You're welcome."

He was grinning like an idiot. "I love you."

"Yeah, yeah. You're just all talk and no action."

"You don't want my action," Trevor pointed out.

"True enough. But nice of you to offer."

"You're very welcome. And seriously, thanks for the slap in the face with a wet dose of reality."

"Just so we're clear, I'm not saying it'll be easy. You'll probably have a few more panic attacks along the way. But from where I'm standing, it seems right. And unless I'm an idiot, the man's not going to leave you ever. Not if he has any say in it."

"I like the sound of that," Trevor admitted, wishing Ollie was already there. "I only—"

He had no idea what he'd intended to say, because suddenly Leah's words were spinning in his head: *not if he has anything to say about it.*

"Bobby," Trevor said, his throat so dry he could barely get the name out. "It's Ollie he wants to punish for being the one Courtney wanted. And now Ollie's on his way here, and—"

"Fuck," Leah said. "I'll call the team and get a lock on his phone so we have a location. You be ready to move the second I have it."

"On my way," he said, already halfway to the garage, the fear that Bobby might get to Ollie first adding fire to his sprint.

"Come on, come on," he said, banging on the dash once he was in and moving through the parking structure toward the street. "Get me the damn coordinates."

And then, just when he feared the call had failed, Leah was back. "Got it," she said. And as she directed him to Ollie's location, Trevor stomped on the gas and tried to tamp down the terror from knowing that he might truly lose the man with whom he'd fallen desperately, hopelessly in love.

\* \* \* \*

Naturally, traffic was a bitch. Then again, it always was in LA. Most of the time that was just background noise. Like the sound of a mosquito that eventually faded into the ambiance.

Right now, that mosquito was buzzing at Ollie's ear, all the more annoying because there was nothing he could do about it.

He started to lay on the horn, but the car in front of him wasn't responsible, and he didn't need to be that kind of asshole.

He was just in a hurry. Why didn't all these Angelinos know he needed to get to Trevor's? Needed to explain to Trevor that he wasn't going anywhere, and the sooner Trevor realized that, the sooner he and Ollie could be together.

Like really together.

Like All The Things together.

He shook his head, then let out a noisy breath. This time not with frustration for the traffic but for himself. Everything that had terrified him about moving forward with Courtney sounded like the most wonderful adventure with Trevor. He wanted on that ride, dammit. He wanted the full Trevor Package.

Before, it had been his own stupid angst and confusion holding them back. Ollie hadn't understood what he wanted. *Who* he wanted. But he did now, and the realization had been one of the best smacks in the face he'd ever experienced.

The frustrating thing was he knew Trevor saw it, too. They were perfect together. And not just sex—although Ollie wasn't about to discount that. No, they'd been friends first, and that had its own kind of intimacy. One that permeated what they had now.

Or, rather, what they *should* have. What Trevor was trying so hard to throw away with both hands, all because that asshole Greg walked away.

But Ollie wasn't going anywhere.

A fact that, sadly, was true in more than one sense of the word. Because he was very, very stuck in traffic.

Well, fuck.

For that matter, fine. Maybe that was an omen. Maybe he needed to take some action to get unstuck.

Damn right, he did.

"Call Trevor," he ordered his phone, then listened as the car filled with the familiar ringtone, then Trevor's voice—but not really Trevor.

"You've reached Trevor Barone. I'm away from my phone but please leave a message." And then the long, irritating beep.

"Hey, it's me. Just calling to tell you that you're an idiot. I love you. You love me. But you're getting in your own way. So stop it, already. You can't waltz into my life, make me love you, and then pull the plug. You're my lobster, dammit. So get your shit together, okay? Because I swear, you can push me away, but I'm just going to keep coming, even if it takes another year. Even if it takes five. So get that through your thick head, Barone. I love you. And I'm not going anywhere."

He drew a breath, then ended the call, leaving his heartfelt rambling message in Trevor's voicemail.

If nothing else, Trevor would realize that Ollie really was crazy in love with him.

Hopefully, it would do some good.

The car in front of him inched forward, then hit the gas and blew through the last of the yellow light, hitting the intersection as it changed to red, and managing to escape from the traffic snarl. Ollie felt like applauding the driver's moxie.

Now he was number one in line, sitting at a red light, watching the traffic pass in front of him on the perpendicular street and above him on the overpass for the 101 freeway.

He bent forward, squinting a bit, trying to discern what he was seeing up there. Was that—

Yeah. Yeah, it was. A person—a man—standing on the 101 beside the concrete side barrier, looking down at the snarled traffic in the Valley.

Ollie frowned. The guy probably had a breakdown and didn't realize that getting out of his car was an incredibly foolish thing to do.

He shook his head, wondering how people could be so clueless. Considering the way people changed lanes in this town, didn't the man know he was risking getting sideswiped even though he wasn't even standing in a lane?

Maybe he did. Because now the man was pressing up against the concrete barrier, practically flattening himself against it as if using it for stability. Ollie grimaced, half of him wishing he could communicate with the man, the other half just watching this inexplicable show.

*Or maybe not so inexplicable.*

The guy had a gun. Ollie couldn't be sure from where he stood, but it looked like a sniper rifle, and he was using the barrier to hold it steady.

*What the fuck?*

A question that changed from curiosity to fear when he realized that the gun was aimed right at him.

And then everything happened at once.

Ollie took his foot of the brake as he jammed the shifter into park and threw himself sideways over the middle console, basically faceplanting in the passenger seat as a gunshot rang out.

But the shot didn't come from the overpass. Instead, it came from the sidewalk to his right.

He started to sit up, but his guardian angel must have been watching out for him, because even as he tensed his muscles to do so, a loud *crack* reverberated through the car, and he was suddenly covered with bits of safety glass, not to mention the fluffy stuff that filled the driver's side headrest, now completely destroyed.

*Fuck, fuck, fuck.*

Another gunshot rang out even as he kept one arm over his head and fumbled for the glove box where his own weapon was stored.

And then there was silence. A moment of blissful silence before utter chaos descended. Horns honking, people screaming, and then a rapid pounding at his passenger side door.

He lifted his head slowly, not bringing it up above the level of the dashboard. Just enough so that he could look up and see who was out there.

"*Ollie!*"

Trevor!

He fumbled for the button to unlock the door, then sat up cautiously, realizing that Trevor wouldn't be standing in the open like that if the threat hadn't been neutralized.

"Bobby?" His voice sounded strange with his ears still ringing.

"I thought I was too late," Trevor said, tugging Ollie into his arms, the console the only thing keeping them apart. "He had you in his sights. I didn't have time to think. To aim. I just fired and I—oh, God, he got off a shot. You could have been—"

"But I wasn't. And you got him with the next one." Adrenaline coursed through his body. "You got him."

Trevor squeezed his eyes shut, his hands clenched into fists in an obvious effort to regain control. When he opened his eyes, Ollie saw only regret, and a sharp wedge of fear sliced into his heart.

"Ollie, I—I'm an idiot. I got all up in my head about Greg and, oh, fuck it."

And then, without another word, he pulled Ollie close and claimed his mouth with his own. A long, slow kiss full of promise and apology, love and heat. Desire and respect. A kiss that melted all of Ollie's fears and fired all of his dreams.

"Wow," said Ollie when Trevor finally broke the kiss.

"You're mine," Trevor said firmly, those dark eyes blazing with passion. "Dammit, Ollie, you're mine."

Ollie grinned, happier than he could ever remember being. "Yeah," he said. "Just so long as you know that you're mine, too."

# Epilogue

Ollie watched as Courtney held a drink in her hand, laughing with Leah, Mario, Nikki, and Bree. They were in Malibu at Damien and Nikki's house, and the whole team from the SSA was there, along with the FBI team under Horowitz, and a half-dozen of Courtney's friends who'd been shocked when they'd heard about the kidnapping a week ago in the local paper and on social media.

Behind him, Trevor slid his arms around Ollie's waist, then brushed a soft kiss over his ear.

"How's she doing?"

"Good," Ollie said. "She's already started with a counselor, and she tells me the nightmares have faded. I think moving helped a lot." He twisted in Trevor's arms so that he could face him. "And she tells me that Leah is a great roommate."

"She is," Trevor said, then released him long enough to spin Ollie around so that they were face to face. "You're better. Except when you're hogging the covers."

"I *so* do not do that," Ollie protested. "You're always yanking at them. I have to yank back."

"Uh-huh."

Ollie fought to hide his grin. Trevor had moved in with him the day after it all went down, and Ollie couldn't remember a time in his life when he felt so content.

"You two look cozy," Jamie said, sliding an arm around Ollie's waist and giving him a hip-bump. Brax and Ryan were with her, deep in a discussion about gun trafficking.

"New case?" Ollie asked.

"New movie," Brax said. "Bullshit ending."

Trevor laughed. "They can't all be as happy as ours."

"True that. How's the house renovation going?"

"Fast," Ollie said, then lowered his voice conspiratorially. "This guy thinks I asked him to move in because I love him. Really, I just love the way he works a nail gun and sander."

"You are so going to pay for that," Trevor said, his eyes dancing with mischief.

"What's he paying for?" Nikki asked, sliding in and taking one of Ollie's hands.

"Suggesting that he only wants me for my renovation skills."

Nikki waved the words away. "Oh, just own it," she said airily. "I only want Damien for his money. And, you know, the sex."

"I heard that," Damien said, stepping up to join them. "I think I'm offended. I always assumed the sex came before the money." He took Nikki's hands and pulled her close.

She glanced over her shoulder and winked at the group. "It does, but I can't tell him that. *Ego,*" she mouthed, making them all laugh, then she squealed as Damien spun her around, only to silence her with a long, slow kiss.

"They make almost as good a couple as us," Trevor said.

"Almost," Ollie agreed, then drew Trevor close for a long, slow kiss of their own.

"I love you," Trevor said, when they came up for air.

"I know. I love you, too." He realized he was grinning like a fiend. But why not? He had everything to smile about. Courtney was safe. Trevor had moved in. And he was desperately, hopelessly in love with his best friend.

As far as he was concerned, the world was pretty much perfect, and he told Trevor as much before kissing him again, this time wild and hot and full of promise for how they'd spend the afternoon once they were back at the house and blissfully alone.

When they finally broke apart—a little dizzy, a lot happy— Brax had moved a few feet away and was staring at his phone, his face awash in something that looked to Ollie like a combination of shock and horror.

"Brax? What is it?"

"A text from Sabrina's sister," he said, referring to his girlfriend who'd been murdered in front of him. He looked up at Ollie, his expression more than a little lost. "I didn't even know she had a sister. But she says she knows who killed Sabrina, and she needs my help to bring them down."

THE END

\* \* \* \*

Interested in seeing more about how Ollie and Trevor became friends … and attracted to each other? Be sure to check out HIDDEN WITH YOU and CHARMED BY YOU.

And don't miss Brax and Samantha's story in ENTWINED WITH YOU!

Finally, you definitely don't want to Ashton and Bree's story, WICKED HEAT!

\* \* \* \*

Also from 1001 Dark Nights and J. Kenner, discover Charmed By You, Memories of You, Cherish Me, Indulge Me, Please Me, Hold Me, Tease Me, Tempt Me, Tame Me, Damien, Justify Me, Caress of Darkness, Caress of Pleasure, and Rising Storm.

Sign up for the 1001 Dark Nights Newsletter
and be entered to win a Tiffany Key necklace.

There's a contest every month!

Go to www.1001DarkNights.com to subscribe.

**As a bonus, all subscribers can download
FIVE FREE exclusive books!**

# Discover 1001 Dark Nights Collection Ten

DRAGON LOVER by Donna Grant
A Dragon Kings Novella

KEEPING YOU by Aurora Rose Reynolds
An Until Him/Her Novella

HAPPILY EVER NEVER by Carrie Ann Ryan
A Montgomery Ink Legacy Novella

DESTINED FOR ME by Corinne Michaels
A Come Back for Me/Say You'll Stay Crossover

MADAM ALANA by Audrey Carlan
A Marriage Auction Novella

DIRTY FILTHY BILLIONAIRE by Laurelin Paige
A Dirty Universe Novella

HIDE AND SEEK by Laura Kaye
A Blasphemy Novella

TANGLED WITH YOU by J. Kenner
A Stark Security Novella

TEMPTED by Lexi Blake
A Masters and Mercenaries Novella

THE DANDELION DIARY by Devney Perry
A Maysen Jar Novella

CHERRY LANE by Kristen Proby
A Huckleberry Bay Novella

THE GRAVE ROBBER by Darynda Jones
A Charley Davidson Novella

CRY OF THE BANSHEE by Heather Graham
A Krewe of Hunters Novella

DARKEST NEED by Rachel Van Dyken
A Dark Ones Novella

CHRISTMAS IN CAPE MAY by Jennifer Probst
A Sunshine Sisters Novella

A VAMPIRE'S MATE by Rebecca Zanetti
A Dark Protectors/Rebels Novella

WHERE IT BEGINS by Helena Hunting
A Pucked Novella

*Also from Blue Box Press*

THE MARRIAGE AUCTION by Audrey Carlan
Season One, Volume One
Season One, Volume Two
Season One, Volume Three
Season One, Volume Four

THE JEWELER OF STOLEN DREAMS by M.J. Rose

SAPPHIRE STORM by Christopher Rice writing as C. Travis Rice
A Sapphire Cove Novel

ATLAS: THE STORY OF PA SALT by Lucinda Riley and Harry Whittaker

LOVE ON THE BYLINE by Xio Axelrod
A Plays and Players Novel

A SOUL OF ASH AND BLOOD by Jennifer L. Armentrout
A Blood and Ash Novel

START US UP by Lexi Blake
A Park Avenue Promise Novel

FIGHTING THE PULL by Kristen Ashley
A River Rain Novel

A FIRE IN THE FLESH by Jennifer L. Armentrout
A Flesh and Fire Novel

# Discover More J. Kenner

### Charmed By You: A Stark Security Novella

Former vigilante-for-hire Simon Barré has one steadfast rule: stay far away from celebrities. Too bad Simon's first assignment at Stark Security is to protect A-list actress Francesca Muratti. He can't even turn down the assignment, as that would be violating his second rule—never fail a woman. Now he finds himself up-close-and-personal with a high-maintenance diva whose flash and sass drives him crazy—but whose touch he undeniably craves.

The world might believe that Francesca Muratti leads a fairy tale life, but the truth is far darker. For years, she's kept a horrible secret about her best friend's death. Now someone is threatening to kill Francesca if she doesn't reveal all. She needs protection, but there's no way she's going to tell the sexy Stark Security agent what she did or why she's being threatened. Which means that in order to survive and protect her secrets, Francesca must pull off the biggest acting job of her career: she's going to have to let Simon close, but not let him see her true heart.

\* \* \* \*

### Memories of You: A Stark Security Novella

Hollywood consultant Renly Cooper is fed up with relationships. His recent breakup with a leading lady played out across the tabloids, and the former Navy Seal is more than ready to focus on his new position as an agent at the elite Stark Security agency. He's expecting international stakes. Instead, his first assignment is to protect one of Damien Stark's friends from a stalker. A woman who, to his delight, turns out to be one of his closest childhood friends.

After a foray into online dating puts tech genius Abby Jones in danger, she needs a bodyguard, and her business partner, Nikki Fairchild Stark, enlists help from Stark Security. When the assigned agent turns out to be her best friend from junior high—and her first crush—she's thrilled to discover he's even more delicious now. She hopes one sexy night can turn into more, but Renly is firmly in the friends-with-benefits camp.

As the threat to Abby increases, she tries to keep her growing feelings for Renly at bay. But as the sparks between them burn even hotter, can they go from friends to lovers when the first order of business is simply to keep Abby alive?

* * * *

### Cherish Me: A Stark Ever After Novella

My life with Damien has always been magical, and never more so than during the holidays, a time for us to celebrate the hardships we've overcome and the incredible gift that is our family. Over the years, he has both protected and cherished me. He has made my life more rich and full than I could ever have imagined.

This year, he's treating me and our daughters to a holiday in Manhattan. With parades and ice skating, toy displays and candies. And, most of all, with each other.

It's a wonderful gift, a trip I will always cherish. But this year, I'm the one with the surprise. And I can't wait to see the look of delight and awe when I finally share my secret with Damien.

But I'm terrified that when danger strikes, it will take a holiday miracle for me to even get the chance.

* * * *

### Indulge Me: A Stark Ever After Novella

Despite everything I have suffered, I never truly understood darkness until my family was in danger. Those desperate hours came close to breaking both Damien and me, but together we found the strength to survive and hold our family together.

Even so, my wounds are deep and wispy shadows still linger. But Damien is my rock. My hero against the dark and violence.

When dark memories threaten to consume me, he whisks me away, knowing that in order to conquer my fears he must take control. Demand my submission. Claim me completely. Because if I am going to find my center again, I must hold tight to Damien and draw deep from the spring of our shared passion.

* * * *

## Please Me: A Stark Ever After Novella

Each day with Damien is a miracle, each moment with our children a gift. And yet I cannot escape the growing sense that a storm is gathering, threatening to pull me away, to rip us apart. To drag me down, once again, into a darkness to which I swore never to return.

I have to fight it—I know that. And I am waging the battle with of all my heart. But it is Damien who is my strength, and we both know that the only way to push away the darkness is for him to fold me in his arms and claim me completely. And for me to surrender myself, once again, to the fire that burns between us.

\* \* \* \*

## Hold Me: A Stark Ever After Novella

My life with Damien has never been fuller. Every day is a miracle, and every night I lose myself in the oasis of his arms.

But there are new challenges, too. Our families. Our careers. And new responsibilities that test us with unrelenting, unexpected trials.

I know we will survive—we have to. Because I cannot live without Damien by my side. But sometimes the darkness seems overwhelming, and I am terrified that the day will come when Damien cannot bring the light. And I will have to find the strength inside myself to find my way back into his arms.

\* \* \* \*

## Tease Me: A Stark International Novel

Entertainment reporter Jamie Archer knew it would be hard when her husband, Stark Security Chief Ryan Hunter, was called away for a long-term project in London. The distance is difficult to endure, but Jamie trusts the deep and passionate love that has always burned between them. At least until a mysterious woman from Ryan's past shows up at his doorstep, her very presence threatening to destroy everything that Jamie holds dear.

Ryan never expected to see Felicia Randall again, a woman with whom he shared a dark past and a dangerous secret. The first and only woman he ever truly failed.

Desperate and on the run, Felicia's come to plead for his help. But while Ryan knows that helping her is the only way to heal old wounds, he also knows that the mission will not only endanger the life of the woman he holds most dear, but will brutally test the deep trust that binds Jamie and Ryan together.

* * * *

## Tempt Me: A Stark International Novella

Sometimes passion has a price…

When sexy Stark Security Chief Ryan Hunter whisks his girlfriend Jamie Archer away for a passionate, romance-filled weekend so he can finally pop the question, he's certain that the answer will be an enthusiastic yes. So when Jamie tries to avoid the conversation, hiding her fears of commitment and change under a blanket of wild sensuality and decadent playtime in bed, Ryan is more determined than ever to convince Jamie that they belong together.

Knowing there's no halfway with this woman, Ryan gives her an ultimatum – marry him or walk away. Now Jamie is forced to face her deepest insecurities or risk destroying the best thing in her life. And it will take all of her strength, and all of Ryan's love, to keep her right where she belongs…

* * * *

## Tame Me: A Stark International Novella

Aspiring actress Jamie Archer is on the run. From herself. From her wild child ways. From the screwed up life that she left behind in Los Angeles. And, most of all, from Ryan Hunter—the first man who has the potential to break through her defenses to see the dark fears and secrets she hides.

Stark International Security Chief Ryan Hunter knows only one thing for sure—he wants Jamie. Wants to hold her, make love to her, possess her, and claim her. Wants to do whatever it takes to make her his.

But after one night of bliss, Jamie bolts. And now it's up to Ryan to not only bring her back, but to convince her that she's running away from the best thing that ever happened to her--him.

\* \* \* \*

### Damien: A Stark Novel

I am Damien Stark. From the outside, I have a perfect life. A billionaire with a beautiful family. But if you could see inside my head, you'd know I'm as f-ed up as a person can be. Now more than ever.

I'm driven, relentless, and successful, but all of that means nothing without my wife and daughters. They're my entire world, and I failed them. Now I can barely look at them without drowning in an abyss of self-recrimination.

Only one thing keeps me sane—losing myself in my wife's silken caresses where I can pour all my pain into the one thing I know I can give her. Pleasure.

But the threats against my family are real, and I won't let anything happen to them ever again. I'll do whatever it takes to keep them safe—pay any price, embrace any darkness. They are mine.

I am Damien Stark. Do you want to see inside my head? Careful what you wish for.

\* \* \* \*

### Justify Me: A Stark International/Masters and Mercenaries Novella

McKay-Taggart operative Riley Blade has no intention of returning to Los Angeles after his brief stint as a consultant on mega-star Lyle Tarpin's latest action flick. Not even for Natasha Black, Tarpin's sexy personal assistant who'd gotten under his skin. Why would he, when Tasha made it absolutely clear that—attraction or not—she wasn't interested in a fling, much less a relationship.

But when Riley learns that someone is stalking her, he races to her side. Determined to not only protect her, but to convince her that—no matter what has hurt her in the past—he's not only going to fight for her, he's going to win her heart. Forever.

\* \* \* \*

**Caress of Darkness: A Dark Pleasures Novella**

From the first moment I saw him, I knew that Rainer Engel was like no other man. Dangerously sexy and darkly mysterious, he both enticed me and terrified me.

I wanted to run–to fight against the heat that was building between us–but there was nowhere to go. I needed his help as much as I needed his touch. And so help me, I knew that I would do anything he asked in order to have both.

But even as our passion burned hot, the secrets in Raine's past reached out to destroy us … and we would both have to make the greatest sacrifice to find a love that would last forever.

Don't miss the next novellas in the Dark Pleasures series!

Find Me in Darkness, Find Me in Pleasure, Find Me in Passion, Caress of Pleasure…

\* \* \* \*

Storm, Texas.

Where passion runs hot, desire runs deep, and secrets have the power to destroy…

Nestled among rolling hills and painted with vibrant wildflowers, the bucolic town of Storm, Texas, seems like nothing short of perfection.

But there are secrets beneath the facade. Dark secrets. Powerful secrets. The kind that can destroy lives and tear families apart. The kind that can cut through a town like a tempest, leaving jealousy and destruction in its wake, along with shattered hopes and broken dreams. All it takes is one little thing to shatter that polish.

Rising Storm is a series conceived by Julie Kenner and Dee Davis to read like an on-going drama. Set in a small Texas town, Rising Storm is full of scandal, deceit, romance, passion, and secrets. Lots of secrets.

# About J. Kenner

J. Kenner (aka Julie Kenner) is the *New York Times*, *USA Today*, *Publishers Weekly*, *Wall Street Journal* and #1 International bestselling author of over one-hundred novels, novellas and short stories in a variety of genres.

JK has been praised by *Publishers Weekly* as an author with a "flair for dialogue and eccentric characterizations" and by *RT Bookclub* for having "cornered the market on sinfully attractive, dominant antiheroes and the women who swoon for them."

In her previous career as an attorney, JK worked as a lawyer in Southern California and Texas. She currently lives in Central Texas, with her husband, two daughters, and two rather spastic cats.

Visit JK online at www.jkenner.com
Text JKenner to 21000 to subscribe to JK's text alerts

# Discover 1001 Dark Nights

### COLLECTION ONE
FOREVER WICKED by Shayla Black ~ CRIMSON TWILIGHT by Heather Graham ~ CAPTURED IN SURRENDER by Liliana Hart ~ SILENT BITE: A SCANGUARDS WEDDING by Tina Folsom ~ DUNGEON GAMES by Lexi Blake ~ AZAGOTH by Larissa Ione ~ NEED YOU NOW by Lisa Renee Jones ~ SHOW ME, BABY by Cherise Sinclair~ ROPED IN by Lorelei James ~ TEMPTED BY MIDNIGHT by Lara Adrian ~ THE FLAME by Christopher Rice ~ CARESS OF DARKNESS by Julie Kenner

### COLLECTION TWO
WICKED WOLF by Carrie Ann Ryan ~ WHEN IRISH EYES ARE HAUNTING by Heather Graham ~ EASY WITH YOU by Kristen Proby ~ MASTER OF FREEDOM by Cherise Sinclair ~ CARESS OF PLEASURE by Julie Kenner ~ ADORED by Lexi Blake ~ HADES by Larissa Ione ~ RAVAGED by Elisabeth Naughton ~ DREAM OF YOU by Jennifer L. Armentrout ~ STRIPPED DOWN by Lorelei James ~ RAGE/KILLIAN by Alexandra Ivy/Laura Wright ~ DRAGON KING by Donna Grant ~ PURE WICKED by Shayla Black ~ HARD AS STEEL by Laura Kaye ~ STROKE OF MIDNIGHT by Lara Adrian ~ ALL HALLOWS EVE by Heather Graham ~ KISS THE FLAME by Christopher Rice~ DARING HER LOVE by Melissa Foster ~ TEASED by Rebecca Zanetti ~ THE PROMISE OF SURRENDER by Liliana Hart

### COLLECTION THREE
HIDDEN INK by Carrie Ann Ryan ~ BLOOD ON THE BAYOU by Heather Graham ~ SEARCHING FOR MINE by Jennifer Probst ~ DANCE OF DESIRE by Christopher Rice ~ ROUGH RHYTHM by Tessa Bailey ~ DEVOTED by Lexi Blake ~ Z by Larissa Ione ~ FALLING UNDER YOU by Laurelin Paige ~ EASY FOR KEEPS by Kristen Proby ~ UNCHAINED by Elisabeth Naughton ~ HARD TO SERVE by Laura Kaye ~ DRAGON FEVER by Donna Grant ~ KAYDEN/SIMON by Alexandra Ivy/Laura Wright ~ STRUNG UP by Lorelei James ~ MIDNIGHT UNTAMED by Lara Adrian ~ TRICKED by Rebecca Zanetti ~ DIRTY WICKED by Shayla Black ~ THE ONLY ONE by Lauren Blakely ~ SWEET SURRENDER by Liliana Hart

COLLECTION FOUR
ROCK CHICK REAWAKENING by Kristen Ashley ~ ADORING INK by Carrie Ann Ryan ~ SWEET RIVALRY by K. Bromberg ~ SHADE'S LADY by Joanna Wylde ~ RAZR by Larissa Ione ~ ARRANGED by Lexi Blake ~ TANGLED by Rebecca Zanetti ~ HOLD ME by J. Kenner ~ SOMEHOW, SOME WAY by Jennifer Probst ~ TOO CLOSE TO CALL by Tessa Bailey ~ HUNTED by Elisabeth Naughton ~ EYES ON YOU by Laura Kaye ~ BLADE by Alexandra Ivy/Laura Wright ~ DRAGON BURN by Donna Grant ~ TRIPPED OUT by Lorelei James ~ STUD FINDER by Lauren Blakely ~ MIDNIGHT UNLEASHED by Lara Adrian ~ HALLOW BE THE HAUNT by Heather Graham ~ DIRTY FILTHY FIX by Laurelin Paige ~ THE BED MATE by Kendall Ryan ~ NIGHT GAMES by CD Reiss ~ NO RESERVATIONS by Kristen Proby ~ DAWN OF SURRENDER by Liliana Hart

COLLECTION FIVE
BLAZE ERUPTING by Rebecca Zanetti ~ ROUGH RIDE by Kristen Ashley ~ HAWKYN by Larissa Ione ~ RIDE DIRTY by Laura Kaye ~ ROME'S CHANCE by Joanna Wylde ~ THE MARRIAGE ARRANGEMENT by Jennifer Probst ~ SURRENDER by Elisabeth Naughton ~ INKED NIGHTS by Carrie Ann Ryan ~ ENVY by Rachel Van Dyken ~ PROTECTED by Lexi Blake ~ THE PRINCE by Jennifer L. Armentrout ~ PLEASE ME by J. Kenner ~ WOUND TIGHT by Lorelei James ~ STRONG by Kylie Scott ~ DRAGON NIGHT by Donna Grant ~ TEMPTING BROOKE by Kristen Proby ~ HAUNTED BE THE HOLIDAYS by Heather Graham ~ CONTROL by K. Bromberg ~ HUNKY HEARTBREAKER by Kendall Ryan ~ THE DARKEST CAPTIVE by Gena Showalter

COLLECTION SIX
DRAGON CLAIMED by Donna Grant ~ ASHES TO INK by Carrie Ann Ryan ~ ENSNARED by Elisabeth Naughton ~ EVERMORE by Corinne Michaels ~ VENGEANCE by Rebecca Zanetti ~ ELI'S TRIUMPH by Joanna Wylde ~ CIPHER by Larissa Ione ~ RESCUING MACIE by Susan Stoker ~ ENCHANTED by Lexi Blake ~ TAKE THE BRIDE by Carly Phillips ~ INDULGE ME by J. Kenner ~ THE KING by Jennifer L. Armentrout ~ QUIET MAN by Kristen Ashley ~ ABANDON by Rachel Van Dyken ~ THE OPEN DOOR by Laurelin

Paige ~ CLOSER by Kylie Scott ~ SOMETHING JUST LIKE THIS by Jennifer Probst ~ BLOOD NIGHT by Heather Graham ~ TWIST OF FATE by Jill Shalvis ~ MORE THAN PLEASURE YOU by Shayla Black ~ WONDER WITH ME by Kristen Proby ~ THE DARKEST ASSASSIN by Gena Showalter

COLLECTION SEVEN
THE BISHOP by Skye Warren ~ TAKEN WITH YOU by Carrie Ann Ryan ~ DRAGON LOST by Donna Grant ~ SEXY LOVE by Carly Phillips ~ PROVOKE by Rachel Van Dyken ~ RAFE by Sawyer Bennett ~ THE NAUGHTY PRINCESS by Claire Contreras ~ THE GRAVEYARD SHIFT by Darynda Jones ~ CHARMED by Lexi Blake ~ SACRIFICE OF DARKNESS by Alexandra Ivy ~ THE QUEEN by Jen Armentrout ~ BEGIN AGAIN by Jennifer Probst ~ VIXEN by Rebecca Zanetti ~ SLASH by Laurelin Paige ~ THE DEAD HEAT OF SUMMER by Heather Graham ~ WILD FIRE by Kristen Ashley ~ MORE THAN PROTECT YOU by Shayla Black ~ LOVE SONG by Kylie Scott ~ CHERISH ME by J. Kenner ~ SHINE WITH ME by Kristen Proby

COLLECTION EIGHT
DRAGON REVEALED by Donna Grant ~ CAPTURED IN INK by Carrie Ann Ryan ~ SECURING JANE by Susan Stoker ~ WILD WIND by Kristen Ashley ~ DARE TO TEASE by Carly Phillips ~ VAMPIRE by Rebecca Zanetti ~ MAFIA KING by Rachel Van Dyken ~ THE GRAVEDIGGER'S SON by Darynda Jones ~ FINALE by Skye Warren ~ MEMORIES OF YOU by J. Kenner ~ SLAYED BY DARKNESS by Alexandra Ivy ~ TREASURED by Lexi Blake ~ THE DAREDEVIL by Dylan Allen ~ BOND OF DESTINY by Larissa Ione ~ MORE THAN POSSESS YOU by Shayla Black ~ HAUNTED HOUSE by Heather Graham ~ MAN FOR ME by Laurelin Paige ~ THE RHYTHM METHOD by Kylie Scott ~ JONAH BENNETT by Tijan ~ CHANGE WITH ME by Kristen Proby ~ THE DARKEST DESTINY by Gena Showalter

COLLECTION NINE
DRAGON UNBOUND by Donna Grant ~ NOTHING BUT INK by Carrie Ann Ryan ~ THE MASTERMIND by Dylan Allen ~ JUST ONE WISH by Carly Phillips ~ BEHIND CLOSED DOORS by Skye Warren

~ GOSSAMER IN THE DARKNESS by Kristen Ashley ~ THE CLOSE-UP by Kennedy Ryan ~ DELIGHTED by Lexi Blake ~ THE GRAVESIDE BAR AND GRILL by Darynda Jones ~ THE ANTI-FAN AND THE IDOL by Rachel Van Dyken ~ CHARMED BY YOU by J. Kenner ~ DESCEND TO DARKNESS by Heather Graham~ BOND OF PASSION by Larissa Ione ~ JUST WHAT I NEEDED by Kylie Scott

*Discover Blue Box Press*

TAME ME by J. Kenner ~ TEMPT ME by J. Kenner ~ DAMIEN by J. Kenner ~ TEASE ME by J. Kenner ~ REAPER by Larissa Ione ~ THE SURRENDER GATE by Christopher Rice ~ SERVICING THE TARGET by Cherise Sinclair ~ THE LAKE OF LEARNING by Steve Berry and M.J. Rose ~ THE MUSEUM OF MYSTERIES by Steve Berry and M.J. Rose ~ TEASE ME by J. Kenner ~ FROM BLOOD AND ASH by Jennifer L. Armentrout ~ QUEEN MOVE by Kennedy Ryan ~ THE HOUSE OF LONG AGO by Steve Berry and M.J. Rose ~ THE BUTTERFLY ROOM by Lucinda Riley ~ A KINGDOM OF FLESH AND FIRE by Jennifer L. Armentrout ~ THE LAST TIARA by M.J. Rose ~ THE CROWN OF GILDED BONES by Jennifer L. Armentrout ~ THE MISSING SISTER by Lucinda Riley ~ THE END OF FOREVER by Steve Berry and M.J. Rose ~ THE STEAL by C. W. Gortner and M.J. Rose ~ CHASING SERENITY by Kristen Ashley ~ A SHADOW IN THE EMBER by Jennifer L. Armentrout ~ THE BAIT by C.W. Gortner and M.J. Rose ~ THE FASHION ORPHANS by Randy Susan Meyers and M.J. Rose ~ TAKING THE LEAP by Kristen Ashley ~ SAPPHIRE SUNSET by Christopher Rice writing C. Travis Rice ~ THE WAR OF TWO QUEENS by Jennifer L. Armentrout ~ THE MURDERS AT FLEAT HOUSE by Lucinda Riley ~ THE HEIST by C.W. Gortner and M.J. Rose ~ SAPPHIRE SPRING by Christopher Rice writing as C. Travis Rice ~ MAKING THE MATCH by Kristen Ashley ~ A LIGHT IN THE FLAME by Jennifer L.

## On Behalf of 1001 Dark Nights,
Liz Berry, M.J. Rose, and Jillian Stein would like to thank ~

Steve Berry
Doug Scofield
Benjamin Stein
Kim Guidroz
Tanaka Kangara
Asha Hossain
Chris Graham
Chelle Olson
Kasi Alexander
Jessica Saunders
Stacey Tardif
Dylan Stockton
Kate Boggs
Richard Blake
and Simon Lipskar

Made in United States
North Haven, CT
07 June 2023